SEDUCED BY You

M.L. YOUNG

Cover Design: © L.J. Anderson, Mayhem Cover Creations

Formatting by Mayhem Cover Creations

INTRODUCTION

This book features alternating points of view. Each chapter is titled with the character whose point of view you are reading from.

Want to receive the first three volumes of my serial series The Stipulation for free? Sign up for my mailing list below and have them delivered right to your inbox. You'll receive new book notifications, free books, giveaways, and much more!

http://eepurl.com/bb6VVb

TABLE OF CONTENTS

CHAPTER ONE

Penelope

So far, my last semester in school had been a boring one. I guess I shouldn't have expected too much, but none of my professors even seemed to be trying to give me a challenge, and trust me, I really needed something to keep my mind occupied right now.

Just over a week had gone by since the incident with Blake. I couldn't even believe what happened. Things had always seemed so perfect with him, even if they were never supposed to be. We were supposed to have something casual—something that would fulfill his needs and in turn, fulfill mine. I knew it wasn't supposed to be serious, but it sure felt that way. He made me think the relationship would become serious, but in reality it was all just a joke.

He wanted to save his ass and he went about it the wrong way. Had he been upfront with me from the beginning and asked me not to say anything about us, I wouldn't have. I would've been disappointed about not getting the internship, but I wouldn't be out to get revenge on a guy I'd just slept with. It was just as much my fault for sleeping with him as it was his for sleeping with me. It was sad to think this entire thing could've been avoided, but instead, here I was.

He'd tried to contact me a few times since that night, but it was to no avail. I never answered any calls or texts, and the one time the buzzer to our apartment went off when I was home alone, I was too scared to answer it or see who it was. I didn't want to take the chance.

It wasn't that I planned on never talking to him again, but I just didn't see how I could right now. He'd hurt me, badly, and it wasn't something I thought I could just bounce back from. Even if I did talk to him again, though, I couldn't imagine it would go well. I did harbor some resentment towards him and was still angry with him, and I hoped those feelings would pass. I wasn't the type of person to hold a long grudge, even if I should.

I sat in class tapping the eraser of my pencil against my bright, empty notebook, as the professor hadn't said anything worthy of taking notes the entire lecture. The class, a communications course that was required for graduation, was as dull as a gray sky in the middle of February. My professor, an older woman likely close to retirement, talked more about her own life experiences than things we actually needed to learn. I didn't think I was alone in my assessment, though, as I peered around and noticed that nobody else had taken any notes, and our professor didn't even seem to notice. That was usually the case in classes I took. It seemed like the professor *never* noticed when you didn't care.

"Any questions?" she asked, as our time together had come close to an end.

She looked around the room as nobody, not even the know-it-alls, raised their hands or asked a question. I could tell she hoped somebody asked something, if not just to hear herself talk again, but her hopes were dashed.

"That concludes our lesson for today. Don't forget that we have a test on Friday. I'll see you all again on Wednesday," she said, before going back behind her desk.

I put my notebook and pencil back into my backpack, as I figured I'd hopefully use them another day. I had a different notebook for each class, and at this rate I was thinking this one wouldn't get ten percent full.

I slung my backpack over my shoulders and headed out of the classroom before turning the corner and hightailing it for the exit. This was my last class of the day and besides, I had somewhere else to be.

I had applied for a couple jobs since Blake and I split, as I knew I'd need some kind of income, no matter what it was, if I were to actually pay any of my bills, which were piling up. One of the jobs called me back within two days and wanted an interview today, a request I was happy to oblige. It wasn't anything special, only a perfume girl at a department store, but I figured it would be fairly easy. The job description said I would offer samples to customers and spritz perfume and cologne around to set a mood and ambiance that would make the customers inquire and in turn, buy from us. It wasn't as good as a tech internship, but I figured that ship had sailed and I was better off just applying for actual jobs when I got out of school.

I took the bus home and sat next to an older man who smelled like piss and booze. His beard, long and scraggly, looked decades old, and the smell emanating from of his body seemed like it had been there equally as long. Luckily my stop soon came and I got off so fast I could've burned holes in my shoes. I knew I only had an hour to get changed, get down to the store, *and* get there early so I could make a good impression.

I quickly ran upstairs, my thighs and calves burning, before locking the door behind me and running into my bedroom. Nicolette was of course still at work, though she said I could take any of her clothes if I needed them. I wore a pair of black pants I already had, plus a blue button-up Nicolette said I could take. It was dressy enough to make a good impression, though not so much so that I screamed corporate job hunter. It was the best I had.

Luckily for me there was a bus route fairly close to the department store. I got off before looking at my phone and seeing that I had only fifteen minutes before my interview. I *always* liked to be early for interviews, no matter how big or small the job would be, as I thought that being professional and making a good first impression was key.

"Hello, can I help you?" an older woman behind the customer service desk asked as I walked up.

"Hi, yes, I'm here for an interview. My name is Penelope Wells," I said.

"Oh, yes, the other candidates are here as well. Please take the escalator up to the second floor and turn right. Walk down and you'll see a waiting area," the woman said.

"Thank you," I said with a smile before walking off.

I felt a knot in my stomach as I realized I would be in yet another scenario with a bunch of other candidates around me. Wasn't there one job or internship I could apply to that *wouldn't* have this happening? Couldn't I be the only one for once?

I rode up the escalator and turned right before walking down the shiny white walkway and finding the area the woman was talking about. There wasn't a signup sheet or anything else for identification, but there were three others already waiting in the chairs, playing with their phones. They didn't pay attention to me, which I thought was a little risky, considering I could be the interviewer walking in. For that reason I sat down, knowing I had about ten minutes left by the time on the wall, and waited patiently without my phone out so I could be the only one to say hello when the interviewer walked in.

As I sat with my bag in my lap, another person walked in and sat down. Then a woman in a pantsuit came in with a clipboard and stood in front of us. I, being the only one without my phone out, was the only person to notice her. I smiled politely and waited for her to speak.

"Hello," she said to everyone else, before they pulled their noses from their phones and shoved them away.

She looked at her clipboard as she hummed to herself before looking back up.

"Penelope Wells, please come with me," she said, before turning around.

I quickly got up and followed her down the hallway, where a bunch of offices were, before she opened the door and let me in. She closed the door behind me, sat behind her desk, and pulled out my application.

I looked at her desk and saw a bunch of family photos in silver frames. She and her kids looked absolutely delightful. She didn't show it now, but I could tell she was a happy woman deep down. I guess working in retail didn't really lend itself to making you all too chipper.

"Hello, Penelope, my name is Karen and I'll be interviewing you today," Karen said.

"Thank you for affording me the opportunity. It's a great store," I said, even though I'd never been here a day in my life.

"So, tell me, Penelope, why do you want this job?" she asked, before looking up at me and taking off her glasses.

"Well, I like to think that I'm great with people. Most people feel comfortable around me, and I'm a great seller. I know the right things to say to get people to buy products without coming off as pushy or salesperson-like," I said.

"This position will likely not have as much interaction with sales as you might've thought. You will mostly be giving out free samples and asking if customers walking by would like to smell the product or receive a free spray," Karen said.

"Oh, I didn't know that. Still, I think that I have the right amount of politeness to know when to push, but I also know when to pull back and realize that the customer wouldn't like any interaction," I said.

"Well, we always want our perfume girls to interact with customers passing by. We don't want them to pull back," Karen said.

"I understand that, but I'm not sure I'm comfortable with that. You see, there have been many times when I've gone through a store and an associate or other person hassled me when I just wanted to get what I came for and get out. Usually I find that people who have a certain look on their face are on a mission, and they're the people to stay away from because you'll only be met with rudeness and coldness. Those who have a confused or interested look on their faces will always find you, and those are the types of people who will buy," I said.

"I see. I also see you're still in school. Is this a position you're looking for short-term, or long-term?" Karen asked.

"I could definitely see myself here for a while," I said, smiling, as I lied through my teeth.

I had no plans of staying here long-term. I knew it might've sounded bad, but I was just looking to get through the rest of school and then get a job that paid many, many times more than this one, which was minimum wage. After all, a good computer science degree just shouldn't go to waste.

"That's good to hear. We like to know that our associates would stay here and be a part of our family for the long-term," Karen said.

Karen asked me a few more questions, mostly about times I'd faced adversity or times I went above and beyond to help a customer, before ending the interview and likely preparing herself mentally for the four other candidates she still had to get through. I stood up, shook her hand firmly, and looked her in the eyes as I thanked her for her time and consideration. She didn't say I had the job, or even how many positions were open, but I figured I had a pretty good shot. Had she been turned off by my comment earlier, I felt like she would've acted differently or ended the interview early. She didn't, though, and we walked out of her office together as she said they'd call me about the job either way.

I checked my phone as I walked onto the escalator and saw that I had a message from Nicolette. I opened it and saw that she asked if I wanted to meet for Thai food when she got off work. I said yes, and to make it easier for her I decided to meet her there instead of making her come pick me up. I really wished I had Gustav on standby right now. He always made things easier.

I had enough time to get home and get changed,

which I definitely wanted to do. Going out on the town in business casual was definitely not me. I went home, changed, put on some more makeup, and left just in time, as the restaurant was about a fifteen-minute walk from our apartment, and I wasn't taking the bus.

The nighttime air was chilly. January was drawing to an end. It had been unusually cold this season, though I guess it was never super warm at night this time of year, either. You always needed a jacket, but now I had gloves and a scarf on too. I saw the weather on my phone earlier saying there might be snow tomorrow, though the chance was low. I really hoped it stayed away. Snow and I didn't mix one bit.

Nicolette was pulling into a space about a block away as I walked up. I stopped, waited, and gave her a hug as she walked up before paying the meter.

"How was the interview?" she asked.

"It was okay. I think I did well, but there were a few other people there for the same job. I guess I did as well as I think I could do," I said.

"No CEO pulled you out, did they?" she asked with a grin.

"Very funny," I said, as we walked into the restaurant.

"Hello, do you have a reservation?" the hostess asked.

"No, we don't," Nicolette said.

"How many are in your party?" the hostess asked.

"Just the two of us," Nicolette said.

"I have a table open. Please follow me," she said, before grabbing two menus and guiding us to our table.

The restaurant, which was dimly lit, had the best Thai food you could get anywhere in the city, at least in my opinion. I opened my menu, which was thickly laminated, and read over the options even though I always got the same thing, which was Pad Thai with chicken and no peanuts.

"Feel like some spring rolls?" Nicolette asked.

"If you're paying," I said.

"Yeah, yeah," she said under her breath.

A busboy came and filled our water glasses before leaving us to talk about our days.

"So, how has work been going?" I asked.

"It's going. A lot of stuff on our plate, but we'll get it done. There's a newer guy in my department who's a moron, though. I think he's going to end up holding us back a little," Nicolette said.

"You haven't, you know, heard from *him*, have you?" I asked nervously.

"Who? Blake?" she asked.

"Yeah," I replied.

"Nope, nothing from him. I hope I don't, either. It'd probably be pretty uncomfortable. How are things between the two of you? Did you talk at all?" she asked.

"He's tried talking to me, but I haven't replied or given him anything to work with," I said.

"Are you ever going to? You had a sweet gig, you know," Nicolette said.

"Yeah, but at the expense of my feelings. I was being used, Nicolette," I whispered.

"Yeah, at first, but things changed. He said so, and so did his friend, from what you told me. I agree that what he did was wrong, but he's obviously sorry. I think you should see him again. Talk to him," Nicolette said.

As we talked, the waitress, a cute Asian girl, walked over with a pad of paper in her hand.

"Hello, my name is May and I'll be your waitress today. May I start you off with a drink from our bar, or perhaps some appetizers?" May asked.

"I think we know what we want. I'll have a Malibu and Diet Cola, please. I'll also have the Pad Thai with chicken," Nicolette said.

"I'll just have water, and also Pad Thai with chicken, but with no peanuts," I said.

"Okay," May said, before taking our menus.

"Oh! And some spring rolls, please," Nicolette interjected.

"Got it," May said with a smile, before walking away.

"Yeah, I don't know. Maybe someday, but not now," I said.

"Well, there's one thing you *have* to do then," Nicolette said.

"And what is that?" I asked nervously. Her schemes were never great ideas.

"Go on RandomMeetX and find a guy," she said.

"I don't think that kind of stuff is for me," I said.

"There's tons of people that use it for dating and not hooking up, you old maid. You can even specify that shit now. Just download the app, make a profile, and talk to some guys. They'll even message you first. It's rare in this city that the woman has to initiate the conversation. Maybe go on a few dates, have some fun, and take your mind off Blake," Nicolette said.

Even though RandomMeetX wasn't exactly my thing, the thought of taking my mind off Blake and seeing another guy was tempting. After all, the best way to get over a breakup or separation is to find someone else who'll make you never think of your ex again. Who knows, maybe I'd even find my future husband.

"Yeah, maybe I'll get it later," I said.

"No, do it now. Here, give me your phone," Nicolette said, extending her hand.

"Nicolette, we're in a restaurant," I said.

"Who gives a shit? Give me," she said.

I took out my phone and instead of handing it to

her, reinstalled the app myself and said I would be the one in charge of it. Begrudgingly, she said okay before helping me through the steps of creating another account. I didn't want to connect it to my social media accounts, for fear that somebody on my friends list would find out, so instead I opted to make an account myself and use my email to login.

After putting together a quick profile, which really didn't seem very in-depth, I was on and a bunch of guys in our area who were in my age range pinged and showed up on a map.

"See, there's so many to choose from," Nicolette said.

"This is all so…overwhelming," I said, as I looked at the plethora of pictures slowing down my phone.

"Don't let it be. You can sort even more if you'd like," Nicolette said, as she pointed and showed me.

I clicked on the tab and additional options came up to drill down the searches even more. I picked height, body type, and even what they were looking for. I took off hook-ups and only put on new friends and relationships, which I thought was pretty good. Nicolette said it was good too, so I hit save and the list of guys became much more manageable. It was amazing how many of them went away, and I was left with a few who looked promising.

"Message someone," she said.

"I thought they'd come to me," I said.

"Yeah, but it might be guys looking to fuck. If you see someone you like, go for it! It's 2015, you shouldn't have to wait for a guy to come to you," Nicolette said.

A notification popped up that a guy on my list had looked at my profile, and I clicked it to go to his. He was a little different than Blake—okay, a *lot* different than Blake, but he looked nice. He was of average height and weight, had glasses, and had just a basic style that looked like it didn't involve a single suit. He was looking for the same things I was, and just as I clicked on his pictures, he messaged me.

"What do I do?" I asked, as I looked at my phone.

"Do you like him?" Nicolette asked.

"I don't even know him," I said.

"No, I mean do you like his profile?" she asked.

"Oh, yeah, it's fine," I said.

"Then open the message," she said, as the waitress brought our drinks and appetizer.

"*Hi, how are you? I don't normally message people on here, but I thought you seemed really nice and you were looking for the same things as me so I thought I'd take a chance. My name is Tyler, and I'd really like to get to know you if you're interested,*" he said.

"He seems nice," I said.

"Loser alert," Nicolette said, dipping her spring

roll into the peanut sauce and taking a bite.

I wrote back, saying it was nice to meet him and I'd like to talk more, before hitting send and putting my phone on silent and back in my bag. Nicolette gave me a weird look before I took my spring roll, which was almost as big as my face, and dipped it in the sauce.

"What?" I asked.

"What if he messages you back?" she asked.

"Let him. I'll get to it later," I said, taking a bite.

"Oh, I see what you're doing," she said, with a big smile. "Playing hard to get, huh?"

"No, I'm just—"

"It's okay, I understand," she said, winking.

I rolled my eyes and ate my spring roll before Nicolette pulled out her phone and showed me some of the guys she'd been talking with. Some were okay, but another was clearly after her ass and nothing more. She was so calm and flirty in her messages, and didn't seem to have any problems talking to any of the guys.

"How are you so good in these messages?" I asked.

"I'm in marketing, Penny. I know how to sell myself," she said.

I sipped on my water, as the busboys were always around to fill it back up. I couldn't even get it down halfway before they were there dumping more in. It was like I was being doted on hand and foot, but I couldn't say I didn't like it. I guess Blake did rub off on me a little.

Our food soon came and I pierced the fortress of noodles with my fork and watched as billows of steam flowed out and floated into the air. I rolled some up on my fork and blew on it as Nicolette, still looking at her phone, did the same.

The flavor danced on my tongue as I tried my best not to just shove my face into the plate and eat it without utensils. It was that good. With my stomach soon full, I pushed my plate forward and said no thanks to the waitress when she came by and asked if I wanted to box the rest of it up. I knew having even a sliver of my original portion back home would only make me crave it more. I was better off just cutting the cord now.

We split the bill, even though Nicolette offered to pay because of my job situation, but I put down thirteen bucks and made her take it.

We walked out of the restaurant and got into her car. As a Pad Thai burp wafted out of my mouth, we drove home, where we would sit around and watch trashy television all night long. It was going to be nice.

CHAPTER TWO

Blake

There are things in life we can't always control. That's a given. For me, though, that just wasn't acceptable.

I'd changed my ways since those days. While I still craved control, I knew that sometimes it wasn't always possible to have what you wanted when you wanted it. Money and power won't always bring you happiness, even though they can sure damn try. I learned that the hard way with Penny. I'd tried to contact her multiple times in multiple ways. I'd called her, texted her, emailed her, and even thought about sending her flowers, though I didn't do that. I just wanted a moment to spend with her to explain myself better and have the closure that would come if I spilled it out there and she still said no. At least I'd know I tried.

Work had gone by slowly, though I was still the shark I'd always been. If anything, the breakup with Penny had made me even more of a shark and led to deals I might not have had before. I shouldn't admit it, but I think it was a way for me to still keep that ounce of control in my life that I so desperately wanted and needed. Maybe it would keep me feeling in power, even if it were a small facet of my life.

I picked up my phone as I got out of a meeting and hoped that I would have something. I did, though it wasn't from her. I unlocked my phone before going to my messages and opening our thread. I scrolled up, past my pathetic attempts at winning her back, and towards the better times. I guess I'd never gotten around to wiping the old texts like I usually did with all my messages in case of a hack, but I was glad I didn't get rid of them. They were important right now.

I started to type as the phone scrolled down and my letters appeared below. It was simple, a "can we talk," but it seemed so much more important than that. How could something so small seem so important?

I sent it, though I think I already knew the answer she was going to give me. It was going to be a resounding no, but I supposed I was prepared for it.

Tom had suggested I take someone out and get my mind off her, but I didn't think it would be that easy. He said if I met someone else who was nice and fun I wouldn't even remember Penny's name later on, but that seemed, I don't know, wrong. After all, what if she did come around and then found out I'd been dating other women? I'd shoot myself in the foot. I guess I'd just have to wait and see if she replied. But I couldn't sit around forever, could I?

There was a knock at my door and in came Grace, who was carrying a stack of files that I knew were presents for me.

"I have some files for the buyout. They want you to go over them and how the company and board plan to merge their services with our already existing ones. They also want you to come up with a few ideas, they said," Grace said, as she set the files on my desk.

"I love that we have the money and influence to buy out other companies, but this is always a pain in the ass. Oh well, I guess it's for the best," I said.

Grace smiled and nodded before walking out and closing the door behind her. I pulled the first file off, which had a whole lot of jargon that I didn't understand and never wanted to. I set the file back on top before kicking my feet up and looking out the window.

I pulled out my phone, opened my special version of the app, and perused the slew of women who presented themselves to me. Maybe it wouldn't hurt to go out to dinner with one. I wasn't going to fuck her, but I could always have somebody to go out with and just talk to. Who knows, maybe things would change for me and Penelope would be nothing more than a distant memory. That was what she was supposed to be in the beginning, right? Okay, I knew that wouldn't happen, but at least I'd get out and stop shutting myself in to work.

I picked out one girl, who was about in the middle between a girl like Penny and the plastic type of girl I always went out with before Penny. I think she'd tainted my taste a little bit. Actually, I *knew* she tainted my taste in women a lot.

I typed a message, nothing special, and within five minutes already had a reply and her phone number, which I thought was a good sign. After looking at her pictures and deciding she looked good enough to be seen with, I sent her a text from a different phone number I had and set up a date for three nights later at some Mexican restaurant she was raving about. I usually went for a little finer dining, but I wasn't averse to trying the local culture and flavors every now and again. After all, great things can come from taking yourself out of your usual comfort zone.

I told her I'd see her there and cut off communication, as I didn't want to sit and chat all day with a girl who appeared to be connected to her phone at the hip. As I stood up, looked out my windows, and looked over my empire, my mind was already being taken away.

Maybe I stood a chance at being normal again.

CHAPTER THREE

Penelope

A few days later I sat in class, bored, before my phone buzzed and I peeked at it. It was Tyler, the guy who'd messaged me the other day on RandomMeetX. We'd chatted a little bit, but nothing too serious. He was nice, but I wasn't positive we were compatible. Still, though, I was holding true to my word and at least getting to know him so I could see if anything was there.

"*What are you doing tonight?*" he asked.

Typing slowly so my professor wouldn't see, I replied, telling him I hadn't made any plans.

"*Would you like to go to dinner? I know this great Mexican place we could go to. Best burritos in town*," he said.

I agreed, saying it would be nice and getting the

name from him so I could meet him there. He offered to pick me up, but I declined, stating how I didn't really know him and would rather meet him on my own before going to that stage. He was very polite and understanding, and quickly backed off the subject, which I appreciated. He said to meet him there at seven-thirty, and he would try to set up a reservation for us.

Blake had texted me the other day, but I never replied. I typed something out, something regrettably long, but I ended up deleting it before I could get myself to send it. Nicolette said I should say something and do to him what he did to me, but I wasn't sure I could bring myself to do it. I wasn't a pushover, but I wasn't a bitch, either. Using him for my own personal gain seemed like it would only hurt us even more down the road if we did patch things up. After all, what if things went back to normal and then he found out I did the same thing to him? I guess he couldn't get incredibly mad at me, but it might put another crack in our trust for one another.

I did have to admit that while he'd been gone I'd missed *other* things about him. Things I couldn't really get from other guys, though I guess I could get a sorry attempt at it. I did miss the sex—a lot. After all, our little arrangement was mostly about it, so going without sex all this time wasn't exactly good for my mind, body, or spirit. I knew he wasn't texting and calling me to get that, but I almost wanted to call him in the same way he used to call me. Just use him for it.

I went back to taking notes and getting hand

cramps, as this professor always said way too much and never seemed to take a breath. I was sure her husband really appreciated that personality trait of hers.

I'd been doing well in my classes so far, with my lowest grade being a B, though it was because I'd forgotten a page of homework that my printer must've never printed out or that I lost, because I'd been on top of things otherwise. Even though it was my final semester, I couldn't celebrate or coast until I knew for a fact that I'd passed everything. How embarrassing would it be to sit here thinking things were great and then fail at the last minute? That would *really* screw up my job plans.

I walked out of class with my backpack slung around my shoulders before my phone buzzed in my pocket. I stopped to the side as dozens of students walked past me and pulled it out to see a number I didn't recognize. Without thinking, I opened it and answered.

"Hello, is this Penelope?" a woman asked.

"Yes, this is she," I replied, putting my finger up to my free ear to drown out the noise.

"Hi, Penelope, this is Karen. We interviewed the other day," she said.

"Yes, hi, how are you?" I asked, as I smiled a little bit.

I knew she'd said they'd call us either way, and I'd been waiting for this call, but I didn't know what she'd say. She didn't sound incredibly happy or thrilled, but then again she didn't seem all too chipper when I met her the other day.

"I was just calling because the other day during your interview I said we'd call whether we'd offer a job or not. Well, I'm pleased to say you made the cut and we'd like to extend an offer for the perfume girl position if you're still interested," Karen said.

I bit my lower lip and smiled profusely as I made a fist and thanked the heavens.

"Yes! I'd love to accept," I said, as I felt a small weight being lifted off my shoulders.

"Great! We'd like to get you into training as soon as possible because we've been without somebody in this position and we want to take the strain off of others who've been filling in. Would you be available to start training tomorrow?" Karen asked.

"Yeah, that should be fine. I don't see any problems," I said.

"Great. Please be here at two. You'll have four hours of training, and please wear black slacks and a white shirt. It can either be a button-up or just a nice white blouse. Come to my office when you get here and I'll get you set up," Karen said.

"That sounds great. Thank you so much for the opportunity, and I'll see you tomorrow," I said.

"Thank you, have a good day," she said.

I hung up the phone and almost broke out in a dance as I quickly pulled up my messages and texted Nicolette. I knew it wouldn't be as exciting as her job, or as when I got a full-time position, but it was still great nonetheless. Now I just needed to make sure I didn't stay out too late tonight. I didn't want to have bloodshot eyes with bags under them.

"Really? That?" Nicolette asked, as I came out in my outfit for my date.

"What's wrong with it?" I asked, as I looked myself up and down.

"It's not good for a date like this, Penny. This is a first date, and it sounds pretty casual. You're wearing a hot dress," Nicolette said.

"Yeah, but all my other clothes suck, remember?" I asked.

"You should've gotten more out of Blake. That's your own fault. Here, at least put this jacket on. It will add a little more depth and cover up your shoulders and arms. That way you look a little more casual without showing too much off," Nicolette said, getting a small jean jacket for me to put on.

I put it on and pulled my hair out before looking at myself again and seeing that she had a point. It did look a little more date-like, and not so much hot-night-on-the-town-like. I guess it was a little much to be wearing at a Mexican restaurant that wasn't exactly expensive.

"Have your condoms?" she asked, as I put my stuff in another bag.

"Nic, I'm not fucking him," I said.

"Hey, it's always better to have them and never use them than to want them and not have them. Take one," she said, before ripping one off a roll and shoving it into my purse.

I left it in, but shoved it far down so it wouldn't accidentally fall out later tonight. Tyler seemed like a nice guy, but I didn't want to give him any kind of impressions about what was going to happen tonight.

I put on my shoes and checked my phone to see Tyler had texted me half an hour before saying he'd see me soon. I sent him a text saying I was leaving soon, though Nic told me I shouldn't and should've just left. She said it was great making guys wonder if you were going to show up or not. I wasn't quite that cruel.

"Well, here I go," I said, as I unlocked the front door.

"Good luck. Don't forget to text me if you need a quick out," Nicolette said.

Nicolette quickly locked the door behind me and I walked out of the building as a blast of crisp, cool air beat against my bare legs. I'd put another jacket on top of the one I was wearing, but even it wasn't strong enough to keep the cool air completely at bay. Maybe there was just no winning as a woman in a cooler climate.

There were people standing outside the restaurant laughing and talking as I walked up. Live music was playing from inside, and as I walked up to the door Tyler stood up and walked over to me.

"Hi!" he said enthusiastically, as if he were surprised I'd showed up.

"Hi, Tyler, how are you?" I asked, as I shook his hand.

"I'm great. Would you like to go inside and get our table? It's a bit chilly out here," he said.

"That would be great," I said with a smile.

We walked inside the packed restaurant, where a hostess wearing all black stood behind a wooden podium with the Mexican flag painted on the front. She took Tyler's name and said our table was ready before grabbing two menus and walking us over. We sat down at a smaller table, one with only two chairs, and opened our menus, not saying a single world to one another.

There were so many choices, as was the usual situation at Mexican restaurants, and I couldn't decide what I wanted. Tyler said he was going to go with the carnitas burrito, which according to the menu was smothered in a creamy cheese sauce, but that seemed a little heavy to me. Nicolette told me to never get some crazy meal you'd get with your girlfriends when you're on a date—especially a first date. It doesn't bode well for the rest of the night, especially if you eat a little *too* much.

"Hola, my name is Carmen and I'll be taking care of you this evening. May I start you off with a Margarita or appetizer?" Carmen asked.

"I'll just have a beer. Whatever you have on special today," Tyler said.

"I'll take a Margarita, please," I said, as I strayed from my usual choice of water.

"Great, that sounds good. I'll have someone bring you some chips and salsa," Carmen said with a smile, before walking away.

"So, have you ever been here before?" I asked.

"Yeah, it's great. The food is awesome. You get a lot of it for a really reasonable price. I love it," Tyler

said.

A busboy came and dropped off some chips and salsa. The place seemed to fill up even more with each passing minute. Who knew cheap Mexican food was so popular with people my age?

Carmen brought our drinks and I took a sip of mine before puckering and feeling it go down. Tyler laughed a little as my eyes welled up and I used my napkin to prevent anything from smearing my makeup. I'd worked too hard making it nice to have a cheap Margarita ruin it.

As we sat there, I was facing the door and casually watching new people come in and out as Tyler told me all about his schooling and how he was going for engineering. I nodded between taking sips of my Margarita, as nothing he said really did that much for me. Still, though, I kept it polite and didn't try to make him feel bad.

While I watched the door, however, the crowd parted like the Red Sea as two people came in. With my glass to my lips and the salt against my tongue, I almost choked on my drink as I saw Blake walk in with a girl.

My mind started to race as I tried to understand what I was seeing. Was I even seeing it at all? Maybe it was a trick my mind was playing on me. After all, I was thinking about him earlier. It could just be somebody who looked fairly similar to him and my mind was just making him the same person. Yeah, that must be it. I must be losing it.

"Oh wow, I can't believe *he's* here," Tyler said, as he turned around to see what the commotion was about.

"What?" I asked, my focus broken.

"Blake Hunter. That's him, he just walked in. He's the CEO of—"

"I know who he is," I said, interrupting him.

"You wouldn't think he'd come to a place like this," Tyler said.

"Yeah, you wouldn't think that. I wonder why he's here," I said.

Blake didn't even recognize me as I stared at him without even so much as breaking my stare. The hostess seated him and his date a little bit away from us. I almost wanted him to see me over here with Tyler. Sure, Tyler couldn't hold a candle to Blake, but the fact that I was here with another man should make him jealous—and that was exactly what I wanted.

"So, tell me about your school," Tyler said.

I kept staring at Blake from across the room as I took another sip of my drink and started to feel its effects. He must've known I was coming here tonight. How, though? Did he hack my phone? Did he put something on it when I was asleep at his place one night? There was no way he'd just showed up here. He was too rich to be coming to a place like this.

"Penelope," Tyler said, as he nudged me.

"Huh? What?" I asked.

"I asked about your schooling. You're almost done, right? Computer science?" Tyler asked.

"Oh, yeah, I'm graduating at the end of this semester. It's a tough program, but it's something I've always been into," I said.

"I think it's great to have women in tech fields like that. It's so male-dominated," Tyler said.

"Yeah, there's a lot of testosterone flying around," I said.

I could barely keep my focus on Tyler and his questions as I kept looking over towards Blake. It was really bugging me that he was here. Sure, he looked good, even if his date looked like a bitch, but why was he here? I wanted to just go up to him and confront him, but I knew that wouldn't look good. I'd look clingy then, though I guess he was the one who'd been texting and calling me, not the other way around.

"Have you guys decided what you're having?" Carmen asked, as both of our menus were closed on the side of the table.

"Yes, I'll have the Big Boy Carnitas Burrito," Tyler said.

"Okay, and for you?" Carmen asked.

"I'll have the regular guacamole burrito with veggies," I said.

"Great choice. Our guac is legendary," she said, before grabbing our menus and walking away.

"So, how long have you been single?" Tyler asked.

"Excuse me?" I asked, as my concentration went back to him.

"Oh, I'm sorry, I didn't mean to offend you. I was just wondering how long you had, you know, been single. It was a stupid question," he said, looking down.

"No, you're fine," I said, as I reached out and put

my hand on his shoulder.

"Sometimes I say stupid things when I like someone," he said.

"To answer your question, it hasn't been all that long, I think. It's complicated," I said.

"I understand that. My last relationship was sort of like that too," he said, before starting off on another tangent.

I looked over towards Blake as Tyler talked and as my eyes found him once again, I felt a knot in my stomach. There he was, across the room, his eyes locked on mine, and I knew he'd seen me. I didn't know if I wanted to throw up or run. He didn't look fazed, not even a tiny bit. I could see his date talking equally as much as mine, though he didn't pay any attention to her, just like I didn't pay any to Tyler.

He took a sip of his water and we both couldn't seem to look away. Well, I couldn't seem to look away, but I didn't know his story. Did he notice I was on a date with Tyler? Did it bother him?

"And anyway, that's how I made the Dean's List," Tyler said, catching my attention.

"That's awesome, Tyler. I've always wanted to myself," I said politely, before putting my hand on his and laughing a little.

I hoped Blake was squirming as he saw me with another man. I wanted to look over, but I knew it would be too obvious. He'd see right through me just like he saw through everyone and he'd know I was just trying to make him jealous. I needed him not to think that. I needed him to think I was genuinely having a great time out with a new guy.

"So, have you ever done anything crazy?" I asked.

"Well, one time I went bungee jumping," Tyler said.

"Bungee jumping! That's great!" I said, laughing, overdoing my performance.

"Yeah, it was a lot of fun," Tyler said, with a smile.

"You're great, Tyler," I said, smiling.

I wanted to look back over at Blake and see how he was doing with all this. I wanted to see him look angry and walk out of this restaurant with his little bimbo, but I couldn't seem to look over at him. I knew it'd be obvious. I needed another way.

Slyly, I dropped my fork on the floor, before looking down and pointing it out to Tyler, so it seemed more real. I bent over, picking it up, and looked upwards towards Blake when I came up so I could see how he was reacting.

He was gone. His date, still sitting there, was smiling and looking at her phone, but he wasn't there. I looked around a little, nonchalantly, but didn't see him anywhere. Where could he have gone?

I turned back around before taking a giant swig of my Margarita and wincing as it went down. I hated the cheap shit. After about a minute, and some whispering nearby, Blake came towards us. I froze in my seat, unsure what to say or do, praying he wouldn't start a scene. That didn't seem like him, though. He was usually pretty calm, cool, and collected in bad situations.

He walked past me, not even looking down at me, though he brushed the back of his hand against my shoulder as he went. I felt shivers up and down my spine just like all the other times he'd touched me. He had a power over me that I just couldn't seem to shake, and oh, did I wish I could.

"He's so cool," Tyler said, as he watched Blake walk towards the bathrooms.

"Can you excuse me for a minute? I have to use the restroom," I said, before patting my mouth with my napkin, grabbing my purse, and getting up.

What in the hell was I doing? Was I tempting fate? I didn't even have to use the bathroom, but I couldn't help myself. It was like my legs were moving, but I couldn't stop them. They had a death wish, I was sure.

"Hello, Penelope," I heard, as I walked up to the women's door.

I stopped in my tracks, feeling shivers up and down my spine as his deep voice resonated through my body. I turned around, slowly, as I saw him leaning against the wall in a tiny corridor that had a few ancient payphones. He looked devilishly handsome, his perfectly crafted and cut suit accenting the muscles I wished I could still touch.

"Why are you here?" I asked.

"I'm sorry?" he replied.

"I know you've been trying to talk to me, but following me here when I'm on a date isn't the way to do it," I said.

"Following you? Is that what you think I'm doing?" he asked with a small laugh.

"Well, yeah, why else would you be here?" I asked in confusion, as somebody walked past me and into the restroom.

"Possibly the reason is that I too am on a date. Did you ever think about that?" he asked.

"You would never come to a place like this," I said.

"I obviously would. I'm here now, aren't I?" he asked.

I didn't say a word as I tried to size him up. He didn't look nervous or apprehensive in any way. He looked confident. It made things a lot harder.

"You know, I've been trying to get a hold of you," he said, as he walked closer.

"I've been busy," I said.

"Too busy to text me back? You know I'm sorry for what happened between us. You know I didn't mean for this to happen," he said.

"I don't know what you do and don't mean anymore, Blake. It isn't black and white to me like it used to be when we were together. You changed," I said.

"I did, and for the better. I went from a give-no-shits asshole who used people for my own gain to a person who genuinely cared for somebody for the first time in ages," he said.

"Yeah, right," I said, turning my head, as another person walked past us.

"It's true, whether you want to believe me or not. You were changing me, and not in a bad way. I fucked up, I know, but sometimes you need to fuck up to see what you really have. Sometimes you need to lose something, somebody, to know what was there," he said.

"What, is this your way of trying to get me back?" I asked.

"I don't know, is it? What do you want from me, Penelope? What more can I do?" he asked.

I had a hard time distinguishing how sincere he was being. He was there, in front of me, spilling his guts out, at least by his standards, and I was the one pushing him away. Didn't I want him back? I knew I did, but I didn't think it would be this soon. We'd barely just stopped things.

He looked at me, waiting for a reply. I knew Tyler was sitting back there waiting for me. There was a great guy, super nice and caring, and happy to listen to me, sitting there with no knowledge of what was happening right now. Would I give up somebody who could turn into something nice for somebody who broke my heart?

"I don't know," I said, clearing my throat.

"Penelope," he said, as he cupped my hips and pulled me closer.

"Blake," I mumbled.

"You can't say you've thrown all your feelings for me away. You like me, I like you, so why are we out with other people right now? Why can't we go back to my place, talk a little, and sort everything out?" he asked.

"I'm here with Tyler," I said, as I looked away.

"It feels like you're with *me* right now, not some kid named Tyler," he said, as he leaned in and whispered in my ear.

I felt the humidity of his breath against my ear and I could almost feel his lips against my pulsing neck. Why was I allowing him to do this to me right now? It was like I couldn't help myself. I couldn't push him away. In a weird way, I wanted it, and *badly*.

"Blake, you know we shouldn't be doing this," I said.

"And why not?" he asked.

"Because," I said.

"Tell me a good reason why and I'll walk away right now," he said.

"Because of what happened between us," I said, as I struggled to get the words out.

"I said a *good* reason," he whispered.

I bit my lower lip in anticipation as I almost waited for him to do something to me. Would he be so brash as to do it in a Mexican restaurant? Was he trying to get me back to his place? I didn't know, but I didn't think I could contain it much longer.

"Finish your date and come back to my place afterwards. I'll have Gustav here in one hour to take you," Blake said.

"And if I come, what am I supposed to tell him?" I asked, pointing at Tyler.

"Tell him you're leaving to be with a real man," Blake said, before walking away and taking out his phone, presumably to call Gustav.

Stunned, I tried to make sense of what had just happened. Was I really going there?

I pulled out my phone and went into my contacts before finding Nicolette and calling her. I knew if anybody could help me through this, it would be her. She had a no-nonsense attitude and would help me find my way through this ordeal.

"What's up? Need me to come get you?" she asked.

"Bigger problem. Blake is here, he was here, I don't know. He talked to me, and now he wants me to leave this guy in an hour to go over to his place. I don't think he just wants to talk," I said.

"Go," she said.

"*What*?" I asked, in shock.

"You can execute the plan," she said.

"What plan?" I asked.

"Playing him. Just like he did to you at first. Give him a taste of his own medicine. Get laid, get some things taken care of, and get some new clothes. I swear, your closet is like a thrift store, and not the kind with vintage couture," she said.

"You know I can't do that," I said.

"And why not?" she asked.

"It's wrong," I said.

"More wrong than him doing it to you?" she asked.

"No, but two wrongs don't make a right," I said.

"Yeah, but this way you can get what you want, reveal what happened, and then get the last laugh. He's not going to leave you over it. Especially after he did it to you first," she said.

Did I dare even try something like that? Was it safe? My life was easier when Blake was in it, and while the job I'd just gotten wasn't horrible, it would be nicer to not work at all and have somebody else pick up the tab. I just felt so classless doing it, though. I wasn't that type of girl.

"God, I don't know. I have to think about it," I said.

"Don't do something stupid, Penny. I'm not saying you have to fuck him, but at least talk to him in a personal setting. It's for the best," she said.

"I'll call you later or text you or something. I need to get back to my table. I think my food is there," I said.

"I won't wait up for you," she said.

I hung up, put my phone away in my purse, and took a deep breath before walking back to the table. Tyler was there, smiling. He hadn't started on his food yet.

"There you are," he said.

"I'm so sorry about that. It was a family emergency and I just couldn't get away from it. I feel so bad," I said, lying through my teeth.

"The food just came, and she said the plates were really hot, so be careful. I got you a water, too, because I know that usually with alcohol you need it. I hope that's okay," he said.

"That's great, thank you," I said, smiling.

Tyler was such a nice guy. He was sweet, caring, kind, intelligent, and a great catch…for someone else. I hated even thinking about leaving here and going out with Blake, and I was leaning towards it. I couldn't help myself. Blake had an allure that Tyler didn't possess. I knew I'd never be happy with him in the long run. He just didn't have that "it" factor that drove me crazy.

We ate our food and had a good time before the check came and I insisted on paying my half. Tyler didn't want me to, saying it wouldn't be good etiquette since he asked me out, but I couldn't let him pay for this food and then go off to see Blake. It wouldn't sit right with my conscience. He eventually relented, but made me promise to let him pay the next time we went out. I didn't say no, opting not to hurt his feelings. We got up, walked out of the building, and he hugged me goodbye. He didn't try to kiss me, which was a good thing, and just as he walked away, a familiar face showed up.

"Good evening, Ms. Wells," Gustav said.

"I missed you," I said, as I got into the back of the car.

"And I you," he replied, with a smile.

CHAPTER FOUR

Penelope

I spent the entire car ride trying to figure out what I was going to do when I got there. Was I going to play it cool and act like nothing really mattered? Was I going to spill it all out, knowing I couldn't actually go through with Nicolette's plan? Or was I just going to forgive him and move on?

Gustav pulled up to a familiar sight, as the garage door opened and he drove into the space. With the door shut behind him, he got out of the car and walked around to my door before opening it for me and helping me out. I had to admit that I missed Gustav more than I should have. I guess having a personal driver was a big perk to seeing a billionaire.

"Have a pleasant evening, Ms. Wells," Gustav said, shutting my door.

"Can I ask you something?" I asked.

"Certainly. What is it?" he asked.

"Has Blake said anything about me recently?" I asked.

"No, I don't believe he has. How come you ask?" Gustav asked.

"No reason," I said, smiling.

"Have a good night," he said.

"You too," I said, before walking over to the elevator.

I buzzed up and Blake cleared me as I stepped inside the elevator, clutch in hand, and rode up to his floor. How could he not say anything about me this entire time? I never expected him to spill his guts, but not even a mention? Not even my name and nothing else? It made me wonder just how much he even missed me.

"So, you decided to come," Blake said, as he stood in front of the elevator doors once they opened.

"You only live once, or so they say," I said, as I walked off.

"Would you like something to drink?" he asked.

"Just a water," I said, as I walked over to the couch.

"I thought we'd go—"

"I'm fine here, thanks," I said, as I interrupted him.

He brought over a bottle of imported water and handed it to me, taking one for himself. I broke open the cap and took a few sips before closing it and setting it on the table in front of me. I looked at him, and he looked at me, as I tried to get inside his head.

"So, you miss me, huh?" I asked.

"Of course. Don't you miss me?" he asked.

"I guess. I've been really busy, so I've had my mind pretty occupied," I said.

"Well, I have missed seeing you," he said.

"What about me did you miss?" I asked.

"Well, just about everything. I missed waking up beside you, going out with you, talking to you, and you know, *other* things," he said, with a smile.

I tried not to say a word as his words clashed with Nicolette's nagging suggestions in my head. Was he just trying to get me naked? How could I trust that he was being sincere? What if he was just saying what he thought I wanted to hear? What if Nicolette was right? What if I just needed to give him a taste of his own medicine? I didn't want to be malicious, necessarily, but rather to just let him know that what he did wasn't cool. It didn't matter as much if he didn't mean to do it in the end. He still did it, and I couldn't just give him a week or two of silent treatment as punishment. I needed to make him feel my pain.

"I think I may have acted rashly," I said.

"Oh?" he said, as he perked up a little.

"I can understand why you did what you did, and although I don't agree with it, I wonder if I acted too hastily and didn't give you a chance to explain yourself. You were right that people deserve a second chance, and that's where I'm leaning right now," I said.

"I have to admit, I didn't think it would go like this tonight. I wasn't expecting you to say that," he

said.

"What can I say? I think you'll find I have a lot of surprises," I said with a smile, before taking a sip of my water.

"I know this is sort of sudden, but would you like to stay over tonight? I think it would be nice," he said.

"I have work in the morning, or else I would," I said.

"Work?" he asked, in a surprised tone.

"Yes, work. The thing people do to make money," I said.

"You don't need that. I told you I'd take care of things," he said.

"Yeah, you said that when we were seeing one another. That ended, so I got a job at a department store," I said.

"Quit it," he said.

"I can't just quit," I said.

"Yes, you can. I'd rather you not work in a place like that. I think after what happened, especially, you deserve to be pampered for a little bit and have things taken care of. If you still want a job upon graduation, that's fine. I understand completely," Blake said.

Did I dare let him do this? I almost felt like I was using and extorting him in a weird way. I knew I wasn't, but I also knew that I wasn't going into this, at least right now, with the purest of intentions. I was doing what other women did to him, and something he didn't care for. He did hurt me in a way that no other man ever had and likely never would, though. I guess I was going to quit that job anyway. I could just let somebody else have it.

"Okay, I guess I can do that. I'm not happy about it, but it's okay," I said.

"So, tell me, what made you decide to come over here tonight?" Blake asked, as he came closer to me on the couch.

"I guess I was interested in what could've been," I said.

"You mean what can be?" he asked.

"Potentially. I don't know yet. After all, you did hurt me pretty badly," I said.

"Let me make it up to you," he said, running his fingers through my hair.

"I'm not sure you can," I said.

"Oh, I think I can, Penelope. I think I can make you feel *good*," he said.

"As good as Tyler?" I asked, looking over at him.

I obviously had never had sex with Tyler or ever wanted to, but Blake didn't know that. He had no idea what I'd been doing since we split, and for all he knew I'd had crazy sex with Tyler every single night. Putting a spike of jealously into Blake Hunter was something I was going to relish.

"So, you slept with him, huh?" he asked.

"I didn't say that. A girl doesn't kiss and tell, does she?" I asked.

"You know, there's only one way to find out how much better I am than him," Blake said softly.

"The problem with that is that I've already been there and done that. There's nothing you can do to surprise me, Blake," I said.

Blake leaned in, his lips close to my ear. I could

feel the humidity of his bated breath against me as I tried to keep myself together. Of course I wanted him, badly, but I wasn't about to give him that ammunition to work with. It was my turn to wield the gun, and I planned on using it.

"Why don't you let me see if I can surprise you?" he whispered.

I bit my lower lip as I looked to the right so he couldn't see my face. He was so fucking charming, even when I didn't want him to be. I hated that he could do this to me, but at the same time, I fucking *loved* it. I knew riling him up was the only way, and I also knew what it meant for me. It meant blow-my-brains-out sex that would keep me satisfied into the next millennium.

Blake's lips softly kissed my neck. I closed my eyes, my skin tingling, as his hand on my bare thigh gave me goose bumps. I tried to stay neutral, not showing my excitement, both mentally and sexually, but I almost couldn't resist. I needed that big dick, and I needed it now.

I turned my head, breaking the seal of his lips against my neck, and he leaned in, his eyes closing, and pressed his lips against mine. I didn't relent, instead pushing back and feeling his tongue wrestle with mine. I could taste traces of salsa on his tongue before I swallowed and took in a little air. His hand, still on my thigh, gripped me harder and I felt his fingers push into my flesh. Fucking Christ, he still had it.

I put my left hand up to his jaw and cupped it, feeling it moving as he kissed me. My hand quickly drifted, running through his hair. I could feel the product glaze my fingers as I gripped it a little. I pulled his hair back a little, making him flash the tiniest smile as I continued to kiss him.

I felt empowered as I climbed into his lap and straddled him right on his couch. I grabbed both of his hands, which tried to wander, and pinned them to the back cushion as I tasted every breath he tried to take. I felt like a black widow about to devour her prey, and for the first time in my life, I felt dominant.

He tried to move his hands away, presumably to grab my ass, but I didn't let him, as I hummed "no" and pushed them back. I could feel his bulge growing in his pants under me as I sat down on top of it and helped it get even bigger.

"Getting big for me?" I asked, as I pulled back.

"Getting *huge* for you," he replied.

I smiled, before letting go of his hands and taking off my jean jacket. I tossed it on the floor as his hands gripped my ass. He pulled me a little closer, and I pushed my hands against the back cushion to keep myself upright.

Stabilizing myself, I slung my arms through the top of my dress and pulled it down past my cleavage before unclasping my bra from behind. I pulled it off, tossed it on the ground, and watched in pleasure as his eyes widened.

"Damn, I missed these," he said, before he went to grab one with his left hand.

"No hands," I said, as I slapped it away.

He put his hand back on my ass with a smile before leaning forward and looking up at me while he sucked on my nipple. I ran my fingers through his hair again as I felt his warm tongue flicker against my hardening nipple. His hands squeezed the life out of my ass before he slapped it and I felt the ripples spread through my cheeks. I smiled, letting out a flirtatious laugh, before pushing his face further into my cleavage.

I could tell he wanted to say something, like asking me where this came from, and quite honestly, I didn't have a good answer. All I knew was there was a fire inside me right now that couldn't be extinguished. I needed him. I needed *it*.

As if he'd had enough, he pushed me onto the couch and mounted me. I spread my legs open as he put himself between them and kissed me. He put his left hand on my cheek as our tongues danced. I felt up and down his body before I started to unbutton his dress shirt, one button at a time. With it open, I felt every bump of his abs like I was discovering them again for the first time. It was like we were discovering something new that neither of us had experienced with the other before.

With my dress hiked up above my spread legs, he pushed my left leg against the cushion and his right hand snuck up under the fabric. With his palm holding down my thigh, his thumb pressed against my clit before starting to rotate.

I let out a soft moan before starting to breathe heavier. I could feel myself getting wetter and wetter the longer he went, as the hairs on the back of my neck stood up straight and my pussy begged for him.

I ran my fingers down his abs before stopping at

his belt buckle and tugging on it gently. He didn't say a word, instead kept kissing me, as I unclasped it and pulled it apart. I grabbed his waistband before unbuttoning his pants and unzipping them, and he leaned back a little and let them fall to the ground. I opened my eyes and peeked down at his bulge in his stone gray boxer briefs, a little of his precum soaking through the front.

I ran the palm of my hand against him as I felt him through his briefs. He was so big, and I, seemingly so small in comparison. I knew I wouldn't have any problems making him fit, especially now. I would do whatever it took to accommodate him. *Every* inch of him.

He pushed my panties to the side before his thick thumb rolled around my lips and got wet off me. He put his forehead against mine, opening his eyes, as I bit my lower lip once more and pulled down his briefs. With them resting just below his balls, I grabbed his shaft and started tugging on it as I felt him grow more in my hand, which I didn't think was possible. He leaned forward, kissing my neck, as he put one knee on the cushion and got closer to me. I reached forward even more, this time with both hands, and wrapped them around his cock's intense girth and length.

He pulled away, my hands leaving him, before getting down on his knees and pulling my panties off. I lifted my ass in the air as he got them past it before he tossed them aside and put my feet on the cushion. I looked down, knowing what was coming next, unable to prepare myself before his tongue flickered against my clit.

"Shit," I moaned.

His tongue moved around me as I felt the vibrations from his soft moans against my skin. His hand moved inwards, his middle finger out, as it pressed against me and slowly entered me. I'd almost forgotten what he felt like inside me, and he wasn't even technically inside me yet. At least not the part of him I wanted, anyway.

My right hand gripped the back of his head as I pushed him a little further in. He didn't relent, instead wrapping his lips around my clit and sucking as I thrust my head back into the cushion. He moaned as he sucked on my clit and I curled my toes before resting my legs on his shoulders. He looked up at me, locking eyes, turning me on even more than I already was.

"I need to taste you," I said, before his mouth left me.

He stood up, his cock as straight as a flagpole. I inched forward to the edge of the cushion and grabbed it like my life depended on it. I looked up at him as I slid it into my mouth and started to push it down as far as I could go.

His left eyebrow rose as he pulled off his dress shirt and tossed it to the side. Letting go, I grabbed the sides of my dress and pulled it up as he helped me get it fully off. The floor-to-ceiling windows must've painted a pretty view for some lucky soul in a building nearby.

I massaged his balls with my left hand as my right had trouble wrapping all the way around him to keep him stable. I pushed down as far as I could go, almost gagging myself, before I peeked down and saw his toes curling in pleasure.

"Finger yourself while you suck my dick," he said.

I let go of his balls and started to feel myself. My pussy was so wet I thought I was dripping onto his leather couch. He reached down, cupping my tits, as he squeezed my nipples just hard enough that I knew he was there. His cock, like candy in my mouth, started to fit perfectly as I almost unhinged my jaw to fit him in.

Blake grabbed my hair and wrapped it around his fingers to keep it away from my mouth and used it to guide me to the speed he wanted. I looked up at him, my eyes wincing, as he pushed his cock down my throat and moaned before pulling it out and letting me gasp for air, a string of white spit connecting us.

"Enough of this," he said, in a deep voice. "I want you."

"Then take me."

"I don't have anything here," he said.

"Here," I said, opening my bag and digging for the condom Nicolette had given me earlier. Was I glad for that.

I shoved it into his hands before he unwrapped it and rolled it down his pulsing cock. I watched the latex stretch to accommodate him. Without even asking to leave the open room, he pushed his thighs against mine and waited as his cock hung over me.

"Spit," he said, as he held out his hand.

Looking up at him with lust-filled eyes, I spit

into his hand before he used it to lube himself up. His latex-wrapped dick now glistening, he kneeled down and pushed the tip against me. My eyes half closed, he started to push into me and stretch every bit of my pussy to hold him.

"Fuck," I moaned, as I spread my legs apart a little further.

"God, you're still so tight," he said, as he looked down.

"Because you haven't been around to make me not tight," I whispered, which only made him even crazier.

My hair swung as Blake started to thrust. Every single push made me accommodate him even more, though I supposed I could attribute a lot of it to the amount of my own lube I was providing. There's nothing in this world like having a sexy man with a big cock fuck you like he paid for it. I guess in some ways, though, Blake *was* going to pay for it.

With my tits bouncing, he reached forward and grabbed my left one as he squeezed it like it was his first time feeling it. I put my hand on top of his, pushing it further in, as we locked eyes and didn't let go.

He leaned forward, pushing my legs back, before his lips, his tasty, strong lips, pressed against mine. We made out passionately as I felt his balls slap against me. Why did I let myself miss out on this? It was almost too good to let go.

"Fuck me harder," I whispered in his ear.

He picked up the pace, his knees bent, as I let out a quick moan every time he pushed himself all the way in. It only lasted for a second, maybe a half of one, and it felt the same blissful way it did the first time I got a taste of it.

"Come on, harder," I ordered, as I saw a surprised look in his eyes that I'd rarely seen.

I wondered how he felt about me telling him what to do. After all, he was Blake Hunter. He was the one always after control, but how did he feel being the one losing it?

He pulled out, sweat dripping down his cut chest and onto the floor. He sat down next to me, grabbed me by the hips and pulled me on top of him, reverse cowgirl style. With my back to him, I reached back and put my hands against him for stability. I hadn't tried this move yet, but I had to admit I saw it once in a porno a few months ago.

He reached in front of him and grabbed his shaft before helping guide it into me. I bent down, sliding onto it, before my lips gripped it and I started to bounce on top of him.

I arched my back as he reached forward and grabbed my hips. My eyes closed, I moaned loudly as I felt his cock inside of me in a way I hadn't quite felt it before. I could feel my juices drip down the remainder of his shaft that wasn't inside me and onto his tanned balls.

"Yes," I moaned.

His hands left my hips before drifting upwards and cupping my jiggling tits. I smiled and bit my lower lip as he put my sensitive pink nipples between his thumbs and forefingers and twisted them gently. I loved it when he played with me like that. It was just the right amount of pain to get me going without hurting me.

His left hand stayed on my breast as his right hand, falling downwards, wrapped around front and he pressed his middle finger against my clit. He rubbed it as I tensed my abs and felt it coming. It was too much for my shy little body. I needed release, and I knew it was coming.

“Don’t stop,” I moaned, as my breathing became shallow.

He didn’t, as he neither picked up speed nor slowed down. He stayed right in the zone, which only set me off further. I felt my body tingling as my pussy, which felt tender to the touch, started to quiver under his control. I bit my lower lip harder, holding back my moans, as I clenched my eyes shut and tensed my abs.

“Fuck, yes,” I screamed, as I slowed down my pace and started to slide off his dick.

My body still on top of his, I felt myself cream as I could barely even support my weight any longer. The surge of ecstasy rushed through my weakened body and I could feel Blake under me trying to hold himself back.

“Shit!” he yelled, as I opened my eyes, my vision a little blurry from my orgasm, and looked down.

Without even being able to get his condom off, his massive load shot into the condom and almost burst it wide open. His shaft pulsed as he pumped his sweet cum out of himself, the tip of the condom ballooning up under the pressure. His balls, curling upwards, emptied as I watched in absolute pleasure.

God, was he something else.

I got off of him as his chest, which was a little red from my hands, dripped with sweat. His eyes had a glazed over look. My pussy red and raw, I leaned in closer to him to get a better look. I cupped his balls, making him squirm a little, as I felt the little bits of fuzz that covered them. Looking at him, I leaned forward and kissed him softly on the lips as I realized what I'd done to him. Maybe this wouldn't be such a bad little arrangement after all.

As the night went on I knew that I had given him something that he really wanted, even if it might not have happened in the way he wanted it to happen. I knew I needed to push the boundaries a little and see how open and willing he really was going to be with me now. There was only one way I knew how to do that.

"So, I have a question for you," I said.

"Yes?" he asked.

"You know how some websites have those wish list features, where you can put on things you want for people to get you?" I asked.

"Of course," he said.

"How about I give you mine so that you can get me a few things? There were some cute clothes on there, as well as some new, soft towels that I just loved," I said, as I ran my fingers through his hair.

"Sounds good. Just get it to me," he said,

without hesitation.

Was it really that easy? I felt more surprised than bad, and that's saying something for me, who Nicolette describes as a goody two shoes. I felt a little bad using him like that, but that's what this was all for, right? Nothing malicious, but a way for me to use him a little so that he knew what it was like. I just hoped I wasn't opening a can of worms that I wouldn't be able to come back from.

CHAPTER FIVE

Blake

There's nothing more satisfying than waking up next to a beautiful woman. There she was, Penelope, completely naked and under the sanctity of my luxurious white silk sheets as they draped over her body and exposed her soft, curved figure. With her arm across me, I felt her warm skin against mine while I lay there and tried to wake myself up.

I still couldn't believe she was here with me. Truthfully, I was starting to wonder if I'd ever even see her again, let alone be *here* with her again. It was almost fate that I ran into her last night at that dive of a restaurant. I owed that girl from the app a thousand thanks for suggesting we go there. It looked like going outside my comfort zone and trying something new really paid off.

I'd seen a change in Penelope, though, that I knew I'd never seen before. She wasn't like a woman scorned, but she was different, and I wasn't sure how I felt about it. She was stern, forceful, and took the control away from me on several occasions last night. She did the same sort of things I did to her when we were first together, but I guess I had it coming. I should just be lucky that she was even here with me at all. It wasn't worth it to nitpick over something like this anyway.

If I knew one thing, though, it was that I wasn't going to let her go this time. I wasn't here to play games or avoid lawsuits. I wasn't trying to save my ass, and I certainly wasn't in this for me. Sure, I wanted pleasure and things done my way, but I'd always been like that. Who isn't? I wasn't going to get those things at her expense, though, and I planned on making sure she knew that.

She wasn't a piece of meat I could just throw around and use for my own endless delight. She wasn't the shy, timid girl I tricked but later on started to fall for. She was a beautiful woman who had absolutely flowered since the first time I met her. I wanted nothing more than to give her the world and make sure she knew that I cared and that I was here. I had no ulterior motives.

Her arm soon left my chest as she rolled over on her side, grumbling a little, her back towards me. Smiling a little, I rolled over as well, before wrapping my arm around her waist and scooting closer in.

"Good morning, "she said softly.

"How did you sleep?" I asked, as I grabbed her

hand and laced her fingers with mine.

"A lot better than at home, that's for sure," she said, with a giggle.

"Thank you for staying over. I really enjoy when you do," I said.

Something had changed a couple weeks ago in my interactions with her. I noticed that I'd been a little sweeter, a lot less crass, and a tiny bit more open than I ever had been before—at least since the incident those years ago.

She brought out this side of me I never thought I'd see again, and I was afraid I was going to lose that side when she left me. I thought I'd eventually revert back to my old ways and persona. Even though she only came back last night, and it hadn't been but just a tiny bit over twelve hours, I couldn't help but feel that even this short amount of time had saved me and started to change me. I needed her in my life, in more ways than one.

"Are you hungry? I could make us breakfast before I have to leave," I said.

"That would be nice," she said, yawning and covering her mouth with the back of her hand.

She rolled over, looking at me. Her messy hair and the bags under her eyes made her even more beautiful in my eyes. I was never one for natural anything, but she'd come to show me that natural was the most beautiful thing of all. *She* was the most beautiful thing of all.

"I'll get it started," I said, giving her a sweet kiss on the lips and rolling out of bed.

She watched me as I walked, the covers up to her

mouth, before she stretched and yawned some more. With the cold floor against my feet, I walked down the stairs and into the pristine kitchen, where I opened my fridge to the stock of pre-made foods I'd ordered the other day. I pulled out some breakfast food, all of it with easy heating instructions, and put pancakes, bacon, strawberries, melon, and some juice and water together before she walked down the stairs in a pair of my pajama pants and one of my old shirts.

"I hope you don't mind," she said.

"Not at all," I said, with a smile.

There was something about seeing a woman in my baggy clothes, especially after a passionate night together, that did wonders for me. I couldn't put my finger on it, but it was one of the sexiest things in the world.

"Whatever you made smells really good," she said, as I brought the food over to the table.

"I only heated it up. I can't take all the credit," I said with a smile.

We sat down, poured some juice, and drenched our pancakes with whipped butter and pure maple syrup that my personal shopper told me I just had to try. After taking the first bite, I was reminded why I'd hired her. It was magical.

"So, what are your plans for today?" I asked.

"Not sure anymore. I was supposed to start that job, but I guess that isn't happening. I should probably call soon to cancel and tell them I can't work there anymore. That'll be awkward," she said.

"Do you have classes? I could have Gustav take you," I said.

"No, not today, thankfully. I guess I can study and do some light homework," she said.

"I hate that I even have to go to the office. It would be great to have a day together, just the two of us," I said.

"Yeah, that would be fun," she said.

I watched her eat and I smiled, though not noticeably. Her shiny hair flowed downwards, falling in her face, before she'd shake her head and get it out of the way. I still couldn't believe I was lucky enough to be sitting across from her again. I knew we could bounce back from this stronger than ever, and I even had hopes that one day, maybe soon, maybe not, we could actually be *together* together. I wanted to keep it private, especially from the media's prying eyes, but I truly saw myself with her and nobody else.

We soon finished our meals and put the dishes in the sink before going upstairs and getting ready. We barely touched one another in the shower, at least not intimately, though we kissed and washed each other off.

I soon had to go to work and she said she'd take the bus home, which I said no to and called Gustav to take her. I opted to drive myself to work today, which I was more than fine with doing in order to keep her off the bus. She deserved a nice mode of transportation.

She kissed me goodbye, her lips lingering, as we stood in the garage. I didn't want to let her go. Her hands gripped my shirt as she did so. She finally let go, and I opened the door to the car and helped her in.

"I'll see you soon," I said.

"You'd better," she replied, before I closed the door and Gustav drove her away.

I couldn't believe how well things were going.

CHAPTER SIX

Penelope

Two days had passed since my night with Blake and things were going very well. I seemed to lose a lot of the stress that had plagued my body, even more than I'd lost after getting that job. Karen wasn't too thrilled that I was unable to take the position, but she thanked me for calling her and not just skipping showing up, which she said had happened a few times before. I guess that was the risk of managing minimum wage employees. Sometimes they just don't care.

I'd studied my ass off, using all of the time I would've spent spraying perfume to study instead, and I knew that my grades were going to increase. Nicolette was impressed with me, mostly that I was able to give Blake a taste of his own medicine, and she made me tell her all about our night together. I, of course, told her we had sex, and she couldn't believe that we did it right there on the couch, especially with the kind of place he had. There was no privacy with the tall windows, but I had to admit that was what made it even hotter. Knowing you might be watched while you're naked and have a dick inside you is exhilarating.

Blake had kept in contact with me, as he told me he had a surprise for me that he wanted to tell me in person. I asked and asked what it was, but he never relented, instead telling me I needed to see him soon if I wanted to know. I hated the tease, but I guess it must have been big.

I'd seen a different side to him, one that had appeared just before we ended things, and I had to admit I liked it. He wasn't a dick like he normally was, and though he still could be dickish, he had this new air about him that was actually a little bit normal. He could cheer up my entire day just by sending me one simple little text.

He wanted me to meet him for lunch in his office, which I thought was a little different. He said he had meetings all day and that Grace, his secretary, would order in food and we could just enjoy each other's company. I wasn't averse to the idea, but I was a little nervous to walk into that building, into those offices, and back into *his* office, with everybody watching and wondering why I was there. I knew nobody would remember me or know who I was, except maybe Sharon, though I couldn't imagine she'd say anything. Maybe she'd just think I was there for another internship interview. Yeah, that was probably it.

I got ready, wearing dark-wash jeans that were a little too tight in the ass and a flowery blue blouse Nicolette was about to throw out because it was, apparently, the wrong season. I thought she was nuts, but she thought I was even nuttier for wanting to be seen in it. Sometimes I wondered how in the hell I became best friends with her.

I grabbed my bag and my belongings and headed outside where Gustav, my faithful friend, was waiting for me. I smiled, he smiled, and I instantly felt at ease, as I knew I was in good hands. He was, bar none, the greatest driver I'd ever been with.

"Good afternoon, Ms. Wells," Gustav said.

"Please, call me Penny. We know each other too well for you to call me that!" I said, before I slipped into the car.

A couple of people on the sidewalk looked at me while I got inside and I wondered what they thought about it. I wasn't in a particularly wealthy neighborhood, but it wasn't dumpy, either. I could just be going to the airport, but I didn't have any luggage.

"Looks like we're headed to the office today," Gustav said, as he got into the driver's seat and buckled himself in.

"Yeah, Blake wanted to have lunch there. I guess he's busy," I said.

"Have you ever been there? It's quite a nice setting," Gustav said, as he pulled out.

"Once, but it was for an internship interview," I

said.

"Ah, so is that how you two met?" he asked.

"Yeah, unfortunately it wasn't on different terms," I said, as I thought back to the potential lawsuit.

"Well, in any case, I know it was for the best," Gustav said.

"How so?" I asked.

"Because you two were brought together. That was the way it was supposed to happen. I firmly believe in fate, and that day, though maybe it was not your perfect moment, was how it was supposed to happen," Gustav said.

"Maybe. I don't know. I think it's just complicated with him," I said.

"It can be, yes, but I think you'll come to find as you spend more time with Mr. Hunter that he's a lot more than meets the eye. He has a heart and spirit about him that is something bigger than you'd imagine," Gustav said.

"Is he a good boss?" I asked.

"The best. He doesn't just have me drive him around. He talks to me, knows me, and has even had dinner with my family. He might have his quirks, but he's a great man," Gustav said.

Gustav's words stayed with me as I thought about the man I knew, but I guess at the same time, I didn't really know him. He was an enigma who could always bring new surprises out of the bag. Even the words out of his mouth could take me totally off guard. It was amazing and frightening at the same time.

After a short drive, we arrived at the building where Gustav drove into the underground parking and pulled around to the elevators. He walked around to the side, opened my door, and held my hand as he helped me out.

"That's the elevator to his floor. It's private, so you won't have to walk through the rest of the building," Gustav said.

"Thank you for driving me," I said, with a friendly smile.

"Anytime, Penny," he said.

I walked up to the elevator, where the guard looked at my identification before saying I was good to go and letting me inside. With nobody else in there, I hit the button for his floor and it started moving. I liked knowing nobody else would see me. I wouldn't mind Nicolette seeing me, since I thought it would be a little fun to embarrass her in front of her work friends, but I was happy to forego that in exchange for the discretion this private elevator provided over using the front entrance.

I soon came to his floor and got off the elevator before walking to his office and seeing Grace sitting behind her desk. She smiled and motioned that I could go in and I walked up to the same large wooden doors that I'd originally walked through when I first met Blake. I hadn't been here since the day of my interview, and it was crazy to think of everything that had changed in that short amount of time. Blake and I had been through a whirlwind romance, one that was heartbreaking and rewarding all at the same time, and here I was again, standing in front of these doors, and I was just as nervous to open them as the first time.

I got over it and pushed the massively heavy doors open as I saw Blake on the phone, with his feet up on his desk, smiling from ear to ear as I walked inside. I closed the door behind me and walked towards his desk as he hung up and got up to greet me.

"I missed you," he said, before kissing me softly on the lips.

"How much?" I asked.

"Tons," he replied.

Feeling a bit of butterflies in my stomach, I put my purse down on the edge of his desk and looked at the spread of food that awaited us. Everything looked gourmet, like always, and featured artisan sandwiches, crisp salads, pastries, and lemon-infused water that came in a crystal-like glass. This really was how the other half lived.

"I hope you're hungry," he said.

"Starved," I replied. "I haven't really eaten today."

"How come?" he asked, with an intrigued tone.

"We're low on groceries. Have to go shopping," I said.

"Nonsense. I'll take care of it," he said.

He went over to his phone, hit a speaker button, and told Grace to call the grocers and have them repeat my order from last time, and to put a rush on it for this afternoon. She said she'd call now, and just like that, it was taken care of.

"There," he said, before sitting down in his

comfortable-looking chair.

"You don't have to do those types of things," I said.

"I know. I want to. It makes me happy to take care of you," he said, before unwrapping a sandwich.

"So, what was this surprise that you had for me?" I asked, as I opened the lid to a Caesar salad.

"Well, I got a call the other day about a business trip in a little over a week. It's two days or so, nothing long, but I was wondering if you wanted to go with me. You'd have to miss classes Friday, if you have any, but we'd also have Saturday and then go home that night," he said.

I was a little surprised that he'd decided to ask me to come along on this trip. I knew it was just a quick business trip and not an actual vacation together, but it meant he trusted me and actually wanted to be there with me. It was a step up for him, that was for sure.

"Where is it?" I asked.

"Seattle. We've been looking into opening offices there, which is why I went there on business last time. They want to finalize the deal," he said.

"I'm sure I could swing that. I've never been to Seattle. Is it nice?" I asked.

"It's beautiful. There's a lot of charm that can't be described unless you see it for yourself. I could plan some things for us to do, and we'd of course have great accommodations and dinners together. I'd have most of the day Saturday to give to you as well," he said.

"It sounds lovely," I said, smiling.

"Great. I'll make the arrangements, and all you have to do is pack a bag and show up," he said.

I bit into the salad, the crisp romaine lettuce snapping between my teeth. The dressing, with hints of anchovies, had a bit of a tang, and the Parmesan cheese was aged and plentiful.

"So, what else do you have planned today?" he asked.

"Not too much. More studying, I guess. I'm glad to be out of classes today. They're not exactly difficult, but sometimes it's hard to just go," I said.

"I had that same problem, but it all worked out for me, I'd say. I know it can be tough to sit there and take it all in, especially if you aren't interested in a particular class, but it's all worth it in the end," he said.

"Yeah, I'm hoping so. I really want to be able to get a job in my field, but there's a lot of competition these days for coders and developers. Some portfolios are so extensive, and mine isn't. It's going to be hard," I said.

"Well, maybe it won't be," he said, before taking a sip of his drink.

"How wouldn't it be?" I asked.

"I'm the CEO of a massive tech company. I could call a few people and get you in somewhere, especially if you're a decent developer. I obviously couldn't have you here, because of the conflict of interest, but I have a lot of friends in this industry," he said.

"I couldn't ask that of you. I'd feel wrong," I said.

"It would only be wrong if you were bad at it and took the job away from somebody more qualified. I know you're good, and you're somebody who deserves that job if you really want it. I'm fine taking care of you, but I know that sometimes people just want to work. I don't know what I'd do without work to keep me occupied," Blake said.

"Yeah, I definitely need a job. Not only because I need and want to get out, but because I just want to try to make a difference with my coding. I want to contribute to something that helps people," I said.

"I understand completely. Once you graduate, I'll make the calls," he said.

I looked at him with a smile. I couldn't believe he was going to do this. It almost made me wonder if I should let him. It was still months away, but I didn't want to feel like I was using him for this. I was going to give him a taste of his own medicine, and wasn't running away from that, but this? This was a lot and I almost felt like I was truly using him for it. Oh well, maybe he'd forget about it later on if I still felt this way. There was no real point in bringing it up now when it was still so far away.

"So, do you have plans this weekend?" he asked.

"Oh, you're not just going to tell me I need to go somewhere with you?" I asked, with a sarcastic smile.

"Those days are long gone. If you're free at all, I'd love to go somewhere with you. Maybe we could go shopping, go to dinner, see a show, or whatever else you want. I'm open to anything," he said.

"Anything?" I asked.

"I'm not sure I like the sound of that," he said.

"There's this new restaurant that opened. Nicolette told me about it one morning after seeing the news. They serve insects," I said, almost laughing.

"*What?*" he asked.

I could see the look of discontent in his eyes. I knew he didn't like it, and I knew it wasn't a place he'd ever go to, and I think that's why I chose it. I liked exercising little bits of control over him every now and then. It showed both him and me that things aren't always up to him.

"Yeah, they make regular dishes, traditional ones, but add insects to them. I guess a lot of people around the world eat insects as a normal diet, though I guess they aren't having them this way," I said.

"So instead of spaghetti and meatballs, I can get spaghetti and slugballs?" he asked, smiling.

"Slugs aren't an insect, you idiot," I said, laughing.

"Hey, you never know," he said with a smile.

As our lunch went on, we laughed, talked, and overall had a good time. I expected him to be a little more stressed out at work, but he seemed calm and collected. Maybe he didn't have a huge workload right now, or perhaps he just knew how to check it at the door when I came in. Either way, I was appreciative.

As our lunch drew to a close, I thought about finding Nicolette and going to visit her. I knew she was coming back from lunch, and if Blake said I could, I wouldn't get either her or me in trouble if I chatted with her for a few minutes.

"I have a question," I said, as I put the lid back

on my empty salad bowl.

"Anything," he said.

"Do you mind if I go visit Nicolette for like five minutes? I just want to say hi, and I've always wanted to see her space here," I said.

"That's perfectly fine. We really encourage mingling here, and we love building an atmosphere that's friendly and fun, while still promoting work. Go for it," he said.

I smiled from ear to ear as I thought about sneaking up on her and scaring her. I knew this spot, right under her armpits, that when squeezed could cause her to yelp and perhaps even pee a little. There would be nothing more fun than messing with her in front of her coworkers. I bet they'd hold it over her head for a while.

"Well, I better let you get back to work so you can make those bucks," I said, as I stood up.

"I'll page Gustav and have him here soon," Blake said.

"No, there's no bother. I'm just going to take the bus home. I don't want to bother him. It's fine," I said.

"At least take a cab instead of the bus. Here," he said, taking out his wallet.

An array of black and platinum cards lined the holders. He took out forty dollars and handed it to me.

"It won't cost *this* much," I said.

"Give the driver a nice tip," he said.

I was unsure on if I should take the money or not. After all, I was doing my plan, but it almost felt *dirty*. I knew that I needed it, and that he didn't even care, but was it right? I guess it was only money to get home. It's not like he was handing me a diamond necklace or anything.

I put the money in my purse and walked around his desk before grabbing him as he wrapped his arms around me. Even though I was teaching him a lesson, there was a great deal of comfort in feeling the warmth of his body around me. It was something I'd never forget, and something I knew could never be replicated anywhere else. Sure, somebody else could hug me, but not the way he did. It was special.

"Have a good rest of your day, babe. Let me know the details about that bug place," he said.

"Will do," I said, before I gave him a few little pecks on the lips, our arms still wrapped around the small of each other's backs.

We let go and I grabbed my purse before walking out and down towards where I originally came in for my interview those weeks ago. I knew what floor Nicolette was on, and just planned on walking around until I found her. I couldn't imagine it would be too hard. The cubicle walls weren't exactly tall.

I went into the elevator and to her floor before walking off and watching as colleagues laughed together, people tossed foam balls at the wall before catching them again, and one guy even strummed an electric guitar that wasn't plugged in.

After walking around for about twenty seconds, I saw my target. Her noticeable brown hair with blonde highlights could almost be seen from space. Her back was to me, thankfully, as I snuck up like a tiger prowling across the jungle floor. I needed to attack my prey, and I needed to not be caught.

I walked up slowly, making sure that my bag and shoes made no noise. She typed on her keyboard as I came up right behind her. I extended my hands as a couple of her coworkers nearby looked over at me before I struck. My hands shot into her armpits, pinching them a little, as she jumped up and let out a shriek. She closed her arms downwards, stopping me from finishing the job, before turning around in her computer chair so fast I thought she'd get whiplash. She looked at me with shocked eyes as I stood in front of her.

"I hate you," she said.

I laughed, causing her to a smile a little bit, as her coworkers started to chuckle at her reaction. It wasn't quite as grandiose as I'd hoped, but it was still pretty great. I thought I'd have it etched into my memory for a little while, at least.

"What are you doing here?" she asked.

"Why do you think? We had lunch," I said.

"Ah, and how was that? Good?" she asked.

"Really good. Going on a trip next week, but I'll tell you about that later tonight. Don't want to spill anything here, you know," I said.

"Yeah, I wouldn't want it getting out for my sake, either," she said.

I hadn't ever tried to use my influence with Blake to benefit Nicolette, though I did mention something once. She was very against the idea, as she wanted to get a promotion because of her work ethic and merit instead of me dropping a few hints and getting her something she didn't deserve. She might be a little prissy sometimes, but she did work hard and she had a lot of integrity, which was something I deeply admired about her.

"I understand. So, how's work?" I asked, leaning against her desk.

"It's going. Just a lot on our projects, but nothing I, of all people, can't handle. I can do it all," she said.

"Yeah, you don't have to tell me again. You're probably the best marketer ever," I said.

"Well, I don't know about the *best*, but I'm pretty damned good," she said, with a smile.

I looked around the office, almost feeling a little sad that I wasn't here working right now. I knew I wouldn't be on this floor had I been granted the internship, but just seeing the atmosphere and the people working here made me a little sad about the entire experience. Having Blake was great, and the things he provided me were amazing, but there was still an emptiness I felt, like I wasn't contributing anything to society or the world as a whole.

I went to school, got good grades, and filled my time exclusively with classes and studying when I wasn't out with Nic or Blake, but what else was there? Blake was going to get me either a job or interview, I still wasn't sure which, at another tech place, but even that wasn't going to be on my own. It wouldn't be based on my merit and effort, but rather his connections and friends. I wouldn't feel like I actually deserved to be at that place. Maybe I'd have to think again about having him say anything. I might be better off in the long run if I tried myself. I'd rather try and fail than have him make a phone call and have an instant job. My integrity was worth too much to me.

"Well, I just thought I'd say hi and see your desk. I've never been up here before," I said, as I picked up a little cat doll that she had next to her computer.

"It's nice, isn't it?" she asked.

"Yeah, it is," I said, before setting her figurine back down.

"Well, I guess I'll see you at home. Don't be afraid to vacuum while I'm gone," she said, with a smile.

"Hint taken," I said, giving her a hug.

"See you in a few hours, sunshine," she said.

I smiled, turned around, and walked back towards the elevators a little slower than I should have and peeked around the floor as I walked. Why couldn't this be me? Why couldn't I be making great friends and have little figurines that my coworkers probably got me on my desk? Maybe someday soon. I guess I had to get through college first.

The elevator made a few stops before getting to the ground floor and back to the flamboyant lobby I walked through for my internship interview that day. I walked past security with the others, out into the street, and hailed a taxi driving by. I gave the driver my intersection, he drove off, and home I went.

The apartment and building were quiet as I walked inside. The door creaked as I opened it, sending a shockwave of sound through the stairwell. It was an interesting building, this one, and the old-world charm of an era forgotten seemed to always remind me of its age when I opened doors or propped slightly stuck windows open.

As I walked up to our floor, I noticed a few packages sitting outside my apartment. I walked up, looked at them, and saw they were all addressed to me. Was this the stuff Blake got me? Did he really go through with it? I hadn't gotten any notifications or texts from him.

I tossed my keys and purse aside as I brought the packages inside and opened them all up. Almost everything I wanted was in here, including some new shirts, pants, and the towels that were on my list. He said he would get the stuff for me, but I never actually believed it. I knew he had a lot of money, but I almost felt a little bad as I sorted through the things and took them out.

After opening everything up, I walked to the fridge and opened it before putzing around the options. There wasn't much, but I guess that was going to be changed later once the groceries Blake ordered came. We did have pineapple mango juice, though, so I took that out and poured myself a small glass. The juice was tart. I puckered a little bit and winced before I was able to tolerate a little more. I always loved the way freshly squeezed fruit juice could do that to you while not turning you off from it at the same time.

I set down my glass on the rolling butcher block we had for extra counter space, before our buzzer went off and somebody was in the lobby.

"Yes?" I asked.

"I have a grocery delivery for a Ms. Penelope

Wells," the man said.

"Okay, come on up," I said, buzzing the door open.

I stood near the door before hearing a couple feet walking up the wooden stairs.

A knock soon came and I opened the door to see two men, one older and one younger, standing there with some canvas bags filled to the brim.

"Hi, are you Ms. Wells?" the older gentleman asked.

"Yes, I am," I said, smiling in a friendly way.

"If you could please sign this, we can complete the order," the man said, before handing me a clipboard with a receipt and a pen.

I signed the receipt and gave it to him, and they were kind enough to bring the groceries inside and set them next to the butcher block. The older man, who must've been pushing sixty, tipped his hat and thanked me. I'd noticed that Blake had given them a fifty-dollar tip. If there was one thing he did, it was tipping well and often. I was sure the delivery guys must fight each other when his name popped up for an order.

I closed the door, locked it, and walked over to the green canvas bags before opening the fridge and freezer and loading the items in. Fresh fruit, vegetables, dry items, and pre-made meals were all stuffed inside every drawer, cupboard, and shelf in this kitchen that was readily available.

I took the bags and stuffed them with a few others from the last order before walking over to the couch with my phone and turning on the television. I knew nothing was on this time of day except maybe a trashy talk show, but what other options did I have? I could study, but I'd already done enough of that.

I soon settled in, grabbing a blanket and making myself comfortable, before my lethargy took over and my eyes started to feel heavy.

Guess it was going to be one of those days.

CHAPTER SEVEN

Penelope

"So, are you staying there tonight?" Nicolette asked, as I put on some earrings.

"Most likely. I usually do when I go out with him," I said.

"How has it been going? Getting what you want?" she asked.

"I don't like to think about it that way. It makes it sound dirty," I said.

"Yeah, cause it is," she said, with a small laugh.

"No, it's not. It's just showing him that it hurts to be used, and then that's it. Besides, it's not like he's really doing anything more for me than he used to," I said.

"You've barely even asked him for anything, but I think you're starting to regret what you have asked for," she said.

"Why do you think that?" I asked.

"I think you're seeing that you're doing to him what he did to you. I think it makes you feel bad and you want to end it and just be with him," she said.

"No way, that's not it all," I said, before gulping a little.

"Hey, I don't blame you. You had your fun, and now it's time to maybe end that game. It's also like you said, you aren't really doing or asking for anything more than he gave you in the past. The only crazy thing is the trip, but he invited you to that and you never even asked to go anywhere. Maybe you should wait until after the trip to say anything, though," she said.

"Yeah, probably. I don't want to upset him. He's been stressed out with this new office thing or whatever it is and the last thing he needs is to go into that upset. It's coming up, so I'll just keep my mouth shut," I said.

"Where is he taking you tonight?" she asked.

"That bug place we saw," I said.

"Are you serious? That's not a place for a date!" she exclaimed.

"Sure it is. It really shows off your adventurous side and lets you see your partner in a new light," I said.

"I think you're crazy. You'll be burping up cricket legs all week," she said.

"Oh, shut up," I said, before slipping on my shoes.

"Are you sure you should be wearing a black

dress to do this? Maybe you should get a khaki vest and some cargo pants," Nicolette said, with a smirk.

"Hey, at least I'm going out tonight, Ms. Social Butterfly. You're just going to sit at home and watch your trashy shows you taped," I said.

"Better than eating a worm," she said, turning on the television.

I cleaned out my bag before rearranging it and putting new things inside. I had mints, my phone, a gold-wrapped condom, my keys, and a toothbrush. I knew I'd have some other clothes to wear at Blake's, and I was even thinking of asking if I could keep some of my things there. It was a big step, but it would make my life a hell of a lot easier. I couldn't fit everything in these clutches.

Blake himself was going to pick me up, which was a nice change of pace from having Gustav come. I loved Gustav, and especially talking to him about his family and his life, but sometimes it's nice to have your guy pick you up alone. I never thought I'd have to worry about that, but I guess it was a new facet of my life.

"Okay, he should be here in a few," I said, as I came out of the room all dressed up.

"Ow, ow," Nicolette howled, as I rolled my eyes.

I grabbed a bottle of water from the fridge before taking a few sips and feeling the ice-cold sensation run down my throat and cool me down. My phone buzzed inside my purse, before I took it out and saw the preview saying he was here. I told Nicolette goodbye and walked out of the door as she stayed on the couch eating half-melted ice cream that was likely going to drip all over.

I locked the door before quickly going down the stairs and out into the lobby. Blake was outside in his red Italian supercar. As I walked out, I could see a few people down the street admiring it. I opened the door, struggling to slide down into the super low-positioned seat. The door, which went upwards, came down with ease as I pulled it closed and Blake quickly locked us in.

"You look beautiful," he said.

"Thank you. You look very handsome, as always," I said.

"I try," he said, with a smile, before giving me a kiss hello.

He had the restaurant location in his GPS and as he pulled out the roaring engine vibrated through my body. With my heart racing, I heard the engine pulse as we whizzed by on-looking pedestrians while they gazed and took pictures with awe. It was only too bad nobody I knew from high school was here to see me right now.

The traffic was horrendous, as a Saturday night date was something many other couples and hopeful singles had in mind. Buses and trolleys drove by, and parking on the side of the street seemed almost impossible. We soon reached the restaurant, which was a little bit of a drive from my apartment, and Blake pulled into a lot not too far away and parked under a bright streetlamp. The lot was guarded with a solid steel fence and barbed wire, and was manned by two security guards in a booth up front.

We got out of the car, he locked the car into

security mode and it chirped, and we walked towards the restaurant hand-in-hand as a small February breeze blew.

Other couples walked hand-in-hand too as we dodged and weaved through the crowds. Nobody seemed to recognize Blake, which was nice, and it was almost like I was out with just some random guy nobody knew. That didn't always happen, and even someone like Tyler knew who he was.

"My dear," he said, as he opened the door to the restaurant.

The restaurant had a modern take on the rainforest in terms of décor. The lighting was dim, there were plants and small trees everywhere, and there were even sounds of the rainforest playing in the background as waiters and waitresses served people sitting in chairs that looked like tree stumps. The tables were made to look like a long centipede. It was cool.

"Hello, may I help you?" a hostess, one of two, asked.

"Reservation for Hunter," Blake said.

Without even looking at her reservations list, she perked up and quickly drew the other hostess to attention.

"Please seat Mr. and Mrs. Hunter at their table," she said.

Mrs. Hunter. Huh. How about that? Neither Blake nor I corrected her, and he didn't even seem to notice, or he did a good job of hiding it. I, on the other hand, almost started beaming from ear to ear as I thought about how good it felt to be called that. The girl didn't think I was just some random girl on his arm. Maybe it was the way he was handsy with me, or maybe she just didn't want to assume. Either way, it made my night, and it had hardly even begun.

The other hostess grabbed two menus and asked us to follow her. We went towards the back, which featured a VIP area that was empty aside from us. The table, which was dimly lit and out of the view of most of the other patrons, wasn't quite as long as the other centipede table, but it still contained all the detail and maybe even a little more, with gold accents between the ridges in its exoskeleton.

"This is nice," I said, as I touched it.

"I like how they stuck to their theme, at least. Can't say I'll love the food," Blake said.

"At least you're trying it. It means a lot that you'd do something like this for me, when it obviously takes you outside your comfort zone," I said.

"Anything for you," he said, before opening his menu.

Smiling, I opened mine and began to skim through the selections. The menu wasn't large by many other restaurants' standards, but it was diverse in both the food and the insects available. Some options let you pick what you wanted, like the create your own stir-fry bowl, while others were set in stone and even had a note that said no bug substitutions would be accepted. I guess just like with wine, you had to pair the perfect insect to your meal.

"Hello, and how are the two of you doing this evening?" a man asked, as he walked up to the table.

"Well, and yourself?" Blake asked.

"I'm great, thank you for asking. My name is Zack, and I'll be serving you tonight. May I start you off with something to drink?" Zack asked.

"I'll have the tropical lemonade," I said, as I pointed to the rainbow-colored picture on the menu.

"A great choice. My personal favorite," Zack said.

"I'll do the same, actually," Blake said.

"Great! I'll be back shortly with your drinks. Please feel free to look over the menu, and if you have any questions, don't hesitate to ask," Zack said, before walking away.

"Wow, you got a lemonade?" I asked.

"Why is that such a surprise?" he asked.

"I didn't think you'd drink something so fruity," I said.

"Well, you ordered it, and I trust your judgment. I can never go wrong with you," he said.

I smiled, though it was a little fake, before we went and looked at the menu again. How could I be doing this to him right now? How could I be so vengeful in wanting to get back at him? Here he was, trying new things and trusting me, and I was giving him a great reason not to do it any more. I mean, hell, I had brought him here mostly because I wanted to exercise a little control and make him uncomfortable.

As I panicked in my seat, Zack soon came back with our drinks and set them in front of us. After asking if we needed some more time, Blake said he was ready and I nodded as well.

"I'll have the Angus burger with crushed

mealworms," he said, with an almost alarmed and disgusted face.

"And for you?" Zack asked.

"I'll have the tropical stir-fry with the crickets, but can I have them headless?" I asked.

"Certainly. I'll get those orders in right away for you guys," Zack said.

"I can't believe you have me eating this stuff," Blake said, laughing a little.

"You'll like it, I know it. I've only heard great things about the food, and the ambiance is incredible," I said.

"So, are you excited for our trip?" Blake asked.

"Yes! It's going to be so much fun, I hope," I said.

"It will be. We'll try to pack as much in as possible during the day," he said.

"What about at night?" I asked.

"I have plenty of plans for you at night in a big, fancy hotel room," he said, before taking a sip of his lemonade.

"Do tell," I replied, before taking a sip myself and trying to hold back my lips from pursing from the tart drink.

"I want to taste you again. All of you," he said.

"Is that a fact?" I asked.

"Very much so," he said.

"Why wait?" I asked, as I paused before speaking.

"So, you're telling me you want some tonight?" he asked, almost perking up a little.

"I didn't say tonight…" I said.

"Wait, you're talking about—"

"Mmhm," I replied, with sultry eyes.

"And how exactly would we go about that?" he asked.

"Bathroom," I said, shrugging.

"What if somebody walks in?" he asked.

"Let them," I replied.

I saw him shift in his seat, as I probably gave him the biggest fantasy he could ever dream of. What guy didn't want sex in random places, and then to get fed immediately after? Not only that, but sex in a public place was pretty much a bucket list item for me, at least since I met Blake. He brought out a confidence in me that I didn't know existed before. Might as well get it done with while I still had an open chance.

"How do we go about this?" I asked.

"The bathrooms are right over there. We can go in, lock the door, and go at it," Blake said.

"So we're just going to walk in?" I asked.

"Why not?" he asked, with a smile.

I nodded in that direction, and the two of us got up and started walking over towards the bathrooms. Scared that somebody was watching us, I didn't even look around to see if the coast was clear. I just walked behind Blake.

The restaurant had a family bathroom, which as we walked in I saw was just a private bathroom that luckily had a padlock. We walked in and the lights turned on, and Blake locked the door behind me and pulled on it to test it. It was locked. He turned to me and I pushed him against the door and ran my hands up and down his sides.

"Feisty, are we?" he asked.

"Shut up and kiss me," I said.

Blake grabbed my waist and flipped me around so my back was pressed against the cold metal door and he ravaged me like I'd wanted him to. His hand ran up my thigh and brought up my skirt as I tasted his saliva and wanted more. His tongue, strong and pink, wrapped around mine as I gasped for air and begged for more.

I quickly unbuckled his pants as my nerves got the better of me. What if people were standing outside this bathroom right now? What if they heard us? I guess I couldn't say that I cared too much. After all, when a girl gets an urge, she needs to fulfill it.

With his belt undone, I grabbed the waist of his gray slacks and undid them before unzipping them and letting them fall to the ground. His cock, which was separated by boxer briefs made from a thin layer of an almost spandex-like material, came right out as I pulled the briefs down past his warm, slightly hairy balls.

"God, I love this cock," I whispered, as I started to jerk him slowly.

He grabbed my skirt and pulled it up before pushing my turquoise panties to the side and starting to rub me slowly.

"I love this tight, wet pussy more than you know," he whispered back.

Hearing his words, I bit my lower lip. I could feel myself creaming up all over his fingers. He slowly inserted his middle finger, his longest one, as I closed my eyes and felt myself stretching to accommodate it. God, he was so big and thick, and I was only feeling his finger inside me. I couldn't wait to actually have *him* inside me.

"Oh, yeah?" he asked, as I got down on my knees and looked up at him.

"Mmhm," I moaned, as I opened my mouth and started to suck his dick.

My tongue ran across a vein on the bottom of his shaft as I gripped the base of his cock with two hands to keep it steady. He put his hands through my hair as he held it back and out of the way before using it like reins to guide me back and forth.

I took a deep breath before starting to swallow his dick like an anaconda on a gazelle, feeling it tickle my throat before I winced, my eyes watering, and let go.

"You're so fucking sexy," he muttered, so nobody outside would hear.

As I squatted, I started to finger myself and look back up at him as our eyes locked and I felt myself tingle a little bit more. Blake brought a sexuality out of me that I never thought possible before. I was shy, timid, and definitely not remotely sexy. With him, though, I felt a fire inside that just could never be extinguished.

I heard the door to the men's bathroom next to us open and close. I smiled at Blake and wondered if the person knew we were in here. Part of me hoped so, but I'd feel differently when we went back out to our table.

"Do you have protection?" he asked.

I pulled his cock out of my mouth before rummaging through my purse that sat on the floor and pulling out the condom. I handed him it and he ripped open the golden wrapper and rolled it down his cock. He grabbed my hands, pulling me up, before flipping me around and putting my hands against the door. Looking back, he pulled my ass out before I arched my back and spread my legs. I put my forearms against the cold door and waited as he brushed the tip of his cock against my dripping wet pussy. He spread his legs further apart before I felt his bulging manhood push inside me.

I gasped, letting out a small moan, before realizing I had to be quiet and biting the inside of my cheeks. He started to thrust as his hands gripped my ass cheeks and hopefully started to leave red marks that I could look at later. With them spread apart, he gripped them harder as his thick cock stretched me out in the best way.

"Yes," I moaned, in almost silence.

"Yeah, you like that?" he asked, in an equally low tone.

"Harder," I said.

He grabbed my hair as his right hand left my cheek and pulled it back as I smiled and asked for more. As if I'd triggered something, he slammed himself into me and sent ripples up my ass, and the entirety of his cock was soon inside me.

"I don't think I can last much longer," he said, surprising me.

This was the shortest amount of time he'd ever lasted, but I couldn't blame him. This was high-risk, and with that came increased horniness that wouldn't just go away. Hell, I was creaming my panties before we even got in here. Just the thought of it was enough to set me off.

"Come for me," I moaned softly.

"Quiet, in case someone hears," he whispered.

"I want them to know you're about to come inside me," I said back.

As if I'd sparked something inside him, his breathing started to grow shallow and I heard soft, sweet moans emanating from his body. I felt every inch of every thrust he gave me. I wanted nothing more than to make him come. After another sixty seconds of thrusting, and his breathing getting so shallow I was afraid I'd have to perform CPR, it finally happened.

He slowed down, as he huffed and puffed and tried to blow my house down.

"Yes," I moaned, as his thrusts slowed.

"I'm going to come," he said.

"Give me all of it," I said, as I looked behind me.

The look on his face was awe-inspiring as he stopped thrusting completely and pumped his load inside the waiting condom. I smiled, biting my lower lip, as I watched him try to hold back his deep moans that would fill the restaurant floor. His cock soon stopped, and he pulled himself slowly out of me. I felt every inch of him leave like I felt it enter. With the condom still on his hard dick, I saw the pool of cum sitting inside. A few beads of sweat formed in his hairline.

"How was that?" I asked, with a devilish smile.

"Amazing," he said, slightly out of breath.

I pulled up my panties and pulled down my skirt

as he pulled off the condom and flushed it down the toilet. He buttoned himself back up as I straightened his shirt and wiped off his forehead with a few paper towels.

"Good as new," I said.

"I feel better than new," he said.

"How should we get out of here?" I asked.

"Go out and back to the table. I'll follow in a couple minutes," he said.

I gave him a soft kiss before exiting the family restroom and not seeing another person in sight outside. I was relieved, and hoped nobody heard us or alerted someone to our presence. It wouldn't be good press for Blake, but then again, maybe it would be. Tabloids would love to hear about a Casanova billionaire who had sex in all the right places.

I walked back to the table that still had our lemonades on it before Zack came over.

"Is everything okay?" he asked.

"Oh, yeah, he just wasn't feeling well. I went with him to make sure he was okay. Always taking care of my guy," I said, with what I hoped was a convincing smile.

"Oh, no problems! My girlfriend is the same way. It makes me feel special. Anyway, your food will be up soon. If his stomach is still bothering him, I can try to get him some ginger ale and crackers," Zack said.

"Thank you so much, Zack. I really appreciate your help and concern. I'll definitely let you know," I said, with a friendly smile.

Zack walked away and Blake came out, before

sitting down and taking a sip of his drink.

"What was that about? Is he suspicious?" Blake asked.

"Not at all. I told him you didn't feel well and I was taking care of you," I said.

"Nice," Blake said, with a smile, as if he were proud of me.

Zack soon brought out our food and I looked at the bits of bug embedded in my stir-fry. I knew it was coming, obviously, but actually *seeing* it right in front of me was completely different.

"Is there anything else I can get for you?" Zack asked.

"Nope, I think we're fine," Blake replied.

"Okay, just let me know if something pops up," Zack said, before walking away.

Blake took off the top bun of his burger and looked it over. Bits of mealworm were broken up and dispersed throughout the meat. He put some garlic aioli on and put the bun back before picking it up and looking at me.

"Scared?" he asked.

"Of this? Please," I replied.

"Then take a bite," he said.

"Okay, no problem," I said, as I wrapped some noodles and vegetables on my fork.

"Bugs too," he said, smiling.

With an expression of disdain, I put a cricket on the tip of my fork and put it up to my mouth.

"Same time," I said.

"Okay. One…two…three," he said.

I put the forkful in my mouth as he sat there

watching me, going back on our deal.

"Ass," I replied, as I bit into the crispy cricket body.

He laughed before taking a bite and making an impressed face. He didn't make a fuss, didn't complain, and made sure I didn't do the same either. I couldn't, though. I invited him here, I had to go, and I teased him about trying new things. I couldn't just put my fork down and call it a day. I had to see this through and eat more than him. If not for my sake, then for women everywhere!

The crickets were surprisingly tame. I ate every single one in the bowl. They weren't chewy or soggy, and were pleasantly crisp. The vegetable and noodle mix complemented them perfectly, as did the mango sauce.

"I have to say, I'm impressed," Blake said, after I ate most of my bowl.

"I told you I could do it," I said, before letting out a small burp.

CHAPTER EIGHT

Blake

Having a nice night out with Penny was starting to become one of my favorite things. I never thought it could happen, but it did, and I couldn't help but love it in every sense of the word.

To me it didn't matter what we did, where we went, who we saw, or anything else. I didn't care if we were at a gourmet restaurant, a dive bar, out shopping, at a movie, or anything else. Hell, we could just go walking by the bay and I'd be more than content, even on a chilly night like tonight. Just as long as I was with her, I was fine.

My feelings for her had grown almost tenfold since we got back together. We were to a point, at least in my mind, that was *better* than when we split up those dreadful days ago. We weren't in a bad place then, but this experience seemed to make us both grow, and I was doing most of the growing. I was such a cold soul before I met her, and if I hadn't come out of my office that morning when she was sitting in my building, I might not have ever changed.

There she was that day, essentially sitting in a glass box, staring at me, as I stared back at her and wondered who in the hell she was. I was so enamored out of the gate by her beauty, though it was unconventional, and I knew I wanted her. My feelings were, of course, carnal in the beginning, but I believe that's how it is under most circumstances. You're attracted to a person's body and physical stature before you're ever attracted to their mind or the essence of the person. When I got to know her, though, I tossed all that aside and realized I was really starting to *like* her.

Every time we were together my feelings grew and grew until I didn't even know what to do with myself. I wasn't myself anymore, and I couldn't say it was a bad thing. It was definitely good, but scary at the same time. I'd had to rediscover the things that made me, me. I'd given up a slice of the control I so desperately craved and instead filled it with a level of trust I hadn't felt in what seemed like ages.

Then, things came crashing down. Even though I still love him, Tom spilled it all, just when things couldn't have been at a worse time. Penny stormed off, leaving me at the party, and I just wanted to scream and throw something through a window. Heartbreak is never a pretty thing.

I mostly stayed at home that week, though I still

consumed myself in my work to try to get over the pain. I thought that if I could just occupy myself long enough I'd get over my feelings for her and move on with my life again. I'd meet some new women, go out to a few clubs, and find someone even better than her. That didn't happen. Instead, I thought about her constantly, sending her a few messages that probably reeked of desperation.

I'd finally given up when I got another chance, and I'd decided not to throw that away. Sure, I still liked being in control, and sure, I probably exerted that sometimes, but it wasn't anywhere near like it was before. She didn't even mention what happened between us, and I wasn't sure if she just didn't want to relive it, or if she'd just moved on and forgiven me for it. She hadn't tried to punish me yet, so that was good—although I might be fine with a spanking or two.

As Penny and I walked out of the restaurant, I grabbed her hand and held onto it for dear life as I looked at her smiling shyly back at me. She always had a way of making me melt a little inside when I made her smile. We walked past scores of people on the sidewalk, none of them recognizing me. The cold air couldn't keep people from going out.

As we approached our lot, which was around the corner, I saw a man sitting on the side of the street with a cardboard sign and a cup, which was halfway full of loose change. He kept his head down, presumably because of the cold, and was bundled from head to toe in wool clothing.

"Here," I said, as I took two twenty-dollar bills

from my pocket.

He looked up, his eyes turning bright, and I almost thought I saw a few tears forming when he noticed what I was handing him.

“Thank you so much, sir,” he said.

I nodded, grabbed Penny’s hand again, and off we went. I caught her looking at me with admiration, as if I’d just ended world hunger, but I didn’t say a word. We got to the car, I unlocked it, and opened her door vertically as I grabbed her hand again and helped her inside. I closed her door, got into my seat, and locked us in as my stallion of Italian engineering roared as loud as a thousand hungry lions before I pulled out and we stampeded off.

We had no other real plans for the night except for going back to my place. It was the go-to place, nothing special, but extremely memorable for the two of us. There was nothing I wanted more than to just hold her and kiss her and never let go. I think that was why I pushed for her to come over as often as I did. I was never like that with past girlfriends or flames. I guess I’d never had the kind of feelings for them that I had for her.

We pulled into my garage and up my special elevator, looking out over the lights of the city while we ascended. I looked over at her, slyly, and saw her big eyes shimmering like diamonds in the light. She was so beautifully perfect. I still couldn’t believe I’d snagged somebody as great as her.

The elevator soon stopped and we got out of the car as the doors opened and walked into my apartment. The floors were sparkling. Rosa, one of my housekeepers, must've cleaned them today.

"Drink?" I asked, as I walked into the kitchen.

"Have any wine?" she asked.

"Of course. All rich guys have wine," I said, smiling.

I grabbed a bottle from the fridge, nothing fancy, and got two glasses before walking over to her and nodding off to the side.

"Where are we going?" she asked.

"The media room. I thought we could watch a movie or something," I said.

"Sounds perfect," she replied.

We walked inside, dimmed the lights, and got into our favorite oversized seats before I uncorked the bottle and poured some in our glasses. The white nectar, a gift from a business partner, tickled my senses before I set my glass down and picked up the remote. We scrolled through a few movies before deciding on a romantic one, which was more her choice than mine. Whatever, though, I was just happy to be here with her right now.

The movie started and Penny, who was at my side, grabbed my hand, pulled her feet up onto the sofa, and snuggled up to me. I smiled, though she couldn't see, before I kissed her forehead as she got even closer to me.

I put my arm around her a few minutes in, and felt a warm feeling in my stomach as she turned to me and kissed me softly on the lips. I didn't want to admit to those types of feelings, but I guess I wasn't ashamed of them anymore. Some might think it's not manly to get butterflies, but I think admitting when you get them is the manliest thing of all.

The movie, which had some humor peppered in around the undying romance, soon ended and we were both left tired and ready for bed. I turned off the entertainment system, set our glasses down, and grabbed Penny's hand as I whisked her away towards the bedroom. She giggled, I smiled, and I even chased her inside as she pranced around so I couldn't tickle her, which I admittedly tried to do.

She got on the bed and I jumped on top of her. Her smile and laughter were contagious and I couldn't help doing it myself. I rolled onto my side, the two of us both still in our date clothes, as I propped my head up with my hand and looked at her. A soft glow from the moonlight outside came in and reflected in her eyes.

I leaned in, kissing her softly, tasting the lingering alcohol on her lips. They tasted as sweet as her, and I only wished I could taste them even longer. With her hand on my jaw, and mine on her hip, we began to make out like hormonal and very horny teenagers who were finally left alone for the first time. It didn't lead to anything, as we'd knocked that out of the park earlier, but I still couldn't help but feel entirely turned on as I kissed the only woman who mattered in my world.

After fifteen minutes we stopped, and she slowly pulled back as our lips still stuck together until the very end. Our eyes opened at the same time, and as I gazed into hers I swore I could see a glimpse of her perfect soul. She smiled, causing me to smile too, as I tried unsuccessfully to hold it back.

"I'm sleepy," she said, as she yawned a little.

"Need some clothes?" I asked.

She nodded and I got up and went into my closet before pulling out some old pajamas and bringing them to her. She slipped off her dress, pulled up my pajama pants, and slipped the old, tattered shirt over top before hopping back into bed.

She might have been in my old pajamas, but she looked like the most beautiful girl in the world. She picked up her phone and checked her email as I slipped out of my clothes and pulled on some black pajama pants that were by far my favorites. As she set down her phone, she looked at me, and as she locked eyes with me she started to smile.

"What?" she asked.

"Nothing," I replied, as I got in bed and under the covers.

"Thank you for today," she said, as she cuddled up to me.

"Thank you for suggesting it. It was a little out of my comfort zone, but I'm glad I tried it. It's always good to try something new," I said.

I extended my arm and she nuzzled herself up towards me as she wrapped her right arm around my torso and put her head on my chest. I tried to control my breathing as my heart rate picked up every time she cuddled up against me. I was like a teenager again with her. I might not want to relive those days, but I couldn't say I minded this all too much.

"Sweet dreams, beautiful," I said.

She squeezed me a little harder and I turned off the lights with the remote before tossing it aside and closing my eyes. This was almost too perfect.

CHAPTER NINE

Penelope

Waking up next to Blake was something that I never wanted to stop. I missed it when I was gone and loved it when I was here. His hard body was warm against my arm as I found myself still wrapped around him like when I went to sleep. Had I moved at all during the night, or was I like this the entire time? All I knew was that I loved being here more than anything in the world.

He was still asleep, his eyes firmly closed. I let go of him and rolled over before grabbing my phone. With my eyes squinted, I unlocked my screen and opened my email app like I did every morning. Five emails loaded, mostly spam or store sale notifications, though one was from my school.

It said that graduation was around the corner and

if we planned on graduating at the end of this semester, we needed to apply for graduation by the end of this coming week. Making a mental note, I exited the app and locked my phone before setting it on the nightstand and cuddling back up to Blake.

I couldn't believe I was so close to graduation. I'd spent so much time in school, and I was afraid to do anything else but school. My entire life had consisted of sitting through class, from kindergarten to college, and I didn't really know anything else. How was I going to cope when quizzes and homework went away? How was my life going to be without stressful finals? What about the friends I'd made and the memories I'd crafted? That would be all I'd have—memories. I knew I'd never get a Masters degree, mostly because of the cost associated with it, so this was really it.

Blake soon opened his eyes and I looked at him before he turned over, squinting, and looked right back at me. He didn't say a word, instead just looking at me, as his eyes softened and I leaned in and kissed him.

"Good morning," I said.

"Good morning," he replied, in a tired-sounding voice.

"Why are you so tired?" I asked.

"I didn't sleep that great last night," he said.

"How come?" I asked.

"Well, I wanted to change positions, but you were still on me," he said.

"Why didn't you just move? I probably wouldn't have woken up!" I said.

"I didn't want to chance it. You looked so peaceful," he said.

Butterflies tickled my stomach and I couldn't hold back my smile. He was so sweet, and he put my needs above his even when he really wanted something. He cared more about my happiness than his, and that really said a lot about the guy he was becoming. It made me even more nervous to tell him what I had to after our trip. It was becoming more and more difficult as these things happened.

"Thank you," I said, smiling.

"Anything for you. Are you hungry? I could use some coffee," he said.

"I could eat something," I said.

We soon got up and went to the bathroom before going downstairs and shuffling towards the kitchen. The sun was bright and plentiful as it shined brightly through the floor-to-ceiling windows. My eyes were half open at first, as they tried to adjust and not be shocked into staying open. Blake opened the fridge, put some food in the microwave, and started coffee for the two of us. I grabbed a glass of water, as I drank some after waking up every morning at home, and smiled as the cool rush of my drink felt as if it were coursing through my veins.

"Should be a few minutes," he said.

"So, you haven't burped up any legs, have you?" I asked.

"Mine didn't have any. *You'd* be the one burping them up," he replied.

"I don't have any stuck in my teeth, do I?" I asked, before smiling.

"Not a single one in sight, thank God," he replied, with a smile.

The food was soon done in the microwave, and Blake pulled out the steamer box and ripped it open. The pancakes, which were steaming, filled the room with buttery aromatics as my mouth started to salivate and beg for a bite.

Blake poured two mugs of coffee, got out the creamer and sugar, and brought it over to the table as I brought the food. He got two plates and silverware before pulling out a tub of freshly cut fruit from the fridge. I picked up three pancakes and put them on my plate before spreading butter around, cutting them into little pieces, and drizzling pure maple syrup over top. I closed my eyes as I took my first bite. I almost thought it was better than one of the orgasms Blake gave me. I didn't tell him that, of course, so I wouldn't hurt his feelings, but it was *damned* good.

"So, what are the plans for today?" I asked.

"I figured we could have a lazy morning and then I have to hit the office for a little bit," he said.

"Do you work every single day or something?" I asked.

"Pretty much. It never stops, but I don't like stopping anyway. You're free to stay here until I come back," he said.

"No, I'll probably just go home and work on some homework or something. Besides, I don't want to sit here all alone. It's big and can get lonely," I said.

"Now you know why I like having you over so much," he said.

"Oh, I thought it was because of my good looks,"

I said, smiling.

"That too," he replied.

"When am I going to see you again?" I asked.

"When do you want to?"

"Soon," I said.

"Then soon it is."

We mostly talked about our days as Blake asked more about school and how I got into coding. I told him about a time when I was introduced to it by a family friend and basically taught myself from tutorials online. I guess it was just a way for me to escape the everyday happenings of my mundane life, and he understood completely. He said that his own life as a kid wasn't too thrilling, but his mother was a housewife and tried to provide everything she could for him, though it wasn't always enough.

She drank every now and again, which was code for often, and while she was a good mother and loved him a lot, it consumed her more times than he could remember. He said he didn't hate or despise her, but he just wished that the circumstances could have been better. He said his childhood was good overall, though, and he didn't have any major complaints.

I loved learning more about Blake and getting to delve deeper into his psyche and discover things about the man I ultimately saw myself with. We weren't dating yet, or at least we weren't boyfriend and girlfriend, but I almost thought he was starting to lean that way. After all, you wouldn't just invite any old girl to come on a business trip with you unless you really liked her and saw some kind of future with her.

Even though Blake and I were technically dating

and seeing each other, I couldn't imagine what it would be like to actually be official with him. Would things change much, or would we pretty much stay like we were now, but just with a title attached? I'd have to take him home to meet my friends and family then, and I couldn't say I'd enjoy that. They could be pretty rough even with guys back home. I couldn't imagine how they'd be with a billionaire.

They'd probably try stupid shit like asking him for money or for a job, and I wasn't looking forward to putting him in that situation. I guess part of that was the reason I barely ever went back home. What's the point of seeing people like that, who only want to use you or get something from you? It was part of the reason I moved so far away and why I only went back once in a blue moon. They all thought I'd turned city since coming here, but I'd gladly take the compliment they meant as an obvious insult. I'd rather be city than what they called country any day of the week.

As I looked at Blake while he read the news on his tablet, I also wondered what things would be like if we ever moved *past* the relationship phase. Well, at least past the boyfriend and girlfriend phase. Would we ever get engaged, or married, or have kids? I didn't want any of that right now, I was too young and I still had my entire career and life ahead of me, but what if it happened? We got along just great, and even though we'd had a few hiccups, and we could possibly have another one soon, I didn't see why we couldn't move towards that. It would certainly be a whirlwind of a romance story. But I knew I couldn't just sit around and be the doting trophy wife that maybe at one point in time he'd wanted. I was pretty sure he'd abandoned that idea once he really got to know me, though. I had no desire to leave a career and life just to sit in this apartment and watch television all day. Nicolette might like that, but not me.

We sat around for the morning as we talked, cuddled, and played a game on his tablet. I took one half of the screen and he took the other as we handled the controls in tandem and tried to beat every level and obstacle the game threw at us. We weren't that successful, but my cheeks hurt so badly from laughing at one point that I thought I was going to get a cramp.

We took a shower together, a long one, as we washed each other's bodies and made out a little. I think both of us had sex on our minds, but neither one of us acted on it, for whatever reason. I guess I didn't want to keep him from work, but I didn't know what his excuse was.

"I have a question for you," I said, wrapped in a towel, as we stood at his double vanity and I dried my hair.

"Shoot," he said.

"Would you mind if I, I don't know, kept a few things here?" I asked, almost cringing, as I feared his answer.

"Well, like what?" he asked.

"Well, like some fresh clothes so I don't have to wear my old ones, maybe some toiletries so I can properly get ready, and just stuff like that," I said.

"That's a big step, having your things in my apartment," he said.

"It's stupid, I know, I just thought I'd ask," I said, feeling a little embarrassed.

"I don't think you're stupid. I think it sounds okay to me. You're right that you should be able to feel clean and comfortable when you're over here. If you want to have things here, then I'm all for it," he said.

I smiled as I looked at him in the mirror and saw my cheeks turn a little red. I couldn't believe he was being so cool about this, but at the same time I guess I couldn't be all that surprised.

We got dried off and dressed and I wore the same *everything* from the night before. Since we were going in opposite directions, Blake had Gustav drive me home, where I saw a messy Nicolette on the couch eating breakfast as she watched some '90s made for TV movie.

"Have a good time?" she asked, as she ate her bowl of cereal.

"Yeah, we had a great time," I said.

"Get laid?" she asked.

"Nic," I replied.

"Come on, you can tell me," she said.

"Maybe. At the restaurant. I don't know," I said.

"You didn't!" she exclaimed.

I laughed and grabbed a bottle of water out of the fridge as she looked at me with an open mouth. I took a swig of water before setting it down and looking back at her.

"I can't believe you. You're just a little tramp now, huh?" she asked.

"I'm a regular little Nicolette," I replied.

"Watch it, bitch. I'll cut you," she said, with a smile.

I sat down next to her on the couch and looked around as the sunlight twinkled in through the half-closed window, illuminating specks of dust that floated throughout the room. Nicolette wasn't watching anything great, though I suppose she never really did, unless *Jersey Shore* counted as great.

"So, what are you doing tonight?" she asked.

"Not sure. Maybe something with Blake, though nothing has been set," I said.

"Go out with me instead," she replied.

"What did you have in mind?" I asked.

"Dancing?" she asked.

"Ugh, you know I can't dance," I said.

"So what, everyone has to learn at some point. It will be fun to just get out," she said.

"Fine, I guess I'll go, but I'm not promising anything. I might just sit there," I said.

"As long as you go with me, I'll be happy. I found out about this new Spanish dance club that's supposed to be a lot of fun. We'll leave at eight," she said.

I sat around and did a few pages of homework and about an hour of studying, then filled the rest of my time with scouring the Internet and looking at what everybody on social media was doing. My days without a job were incredibly boring, though I guess in a way it was better to sit around and watch TV and go on the computer all day than to stand and spray my thousandth perfume sample in some woman's face. I was sure I would've ended up getting really sick of that very fast.

I didn't put all that much effort into my appearance for dancing—at least not in comparison to Nicolette. She dressed herself completely up, even the makeup and hair, and had painted her nails and toes earlier to match her outfit, which I thought was a little overboard. I guess she was just an overboard type of girl.

"Can't you at least *try* to make an effort?" she asked.

"I don't even know why I'm going. I have a man," I said.

"Yeah, but I don't, and I'm not going alone and looking like a loser. It's not like you have anything better to do," she said.

Blake said earlier that he had a business dinner to go to, which I said was fine because I was being dragged to the dance club. He said to be careful, and not to take a drink from *anyone* besides the bartender. I never really drank anyway, and planned to put a bottle of water in my purse just in case.

Nicolette made me put on a little more makeup and some new shoes before we were ready to hit the town, which were her words and not mine.

Nicolette had called a cab because she said she planned on drinking and I guess assumed I would be too. She paid the fare, so I didn't care how we got there. Our driver, a woman about fifty years old, picked us up outside and took off for the club. She drove like a bat out of hell, weaving in and out of traffic while cursing at anyone and anything that got in her way. That was in between flicking them off and challenging them to fight her, though she never yelled that part quite as loudly, likely for fear that somebody would take her up on her offer.

Nicolette gave her a generous tip, probably because she was scared for her life, before we got out of the cab and she took off again before Nic could get the door fully closed. I brushed myself off and we walked up to the club, where the noxious odor of sweat and horny bodies filled the air. A guy all in black sat on a stool outside. There wasn't a line, but it didn't sound like they had any problems with attendance. We walked up to the gentleman and he nodded for us to go in without saying a word. As we did, I was immediately hit with the humidity of a South American rainforest.

"Nic, this is a little much," I shouted. The music was so loud I could barely hear a thing.

The Spanish music raged as bodies spun around on the dance floor. Plenty of others above, where we were, sat at dimly lit tables and laughed as they drank fruity drinks and tried to seduce the opposite sex.

"Come on, over here," she said, as she pointed towards an empty table.

The table, which was tall and not so large, had two stools that were high enough to make my feet hover in the air. After we sat down, a waitress dressed in almost flamenco-like gear walked up and placed two small napkins on the table.

"What can I get you two ladies?" she asked.

"Two Margaritas on the rocks with extra salt," Nicolette said.

"Oh, I don't—" I said.

"Great, be right back!" the waitress said, before walking away.

"I don't want any alcohol, Nic," I said.

"Oh stop, you need to loosen up. We're at a dance club. There's tons of hot guys around," she said, as she looked down at the dance floor.

The music wasn't all that horrible. I was just glad it wasn't club music like at traditional places. The bodies were plentiful, as men were on women, women were on other women, and men were on other men. They certainly didn't discriminate here, but I guess we *were* in San Francisco.

The waitress came back with our drinks and Nicolette handed her some cash as she graciously said thank you and left. I mixed my drink with a skinny black stirrer before looking up at Nicolette, who was already taking her first chug. I rolled my eyes and took a sip of my own, the tart liquid making me pucker my lips as my eyes welled up.

"Shit," I said, as I set it down.

"They're good, huh?" she asked.

"Yeah, if you like to drink jet fuel," I said.

After about five minutes of sitting there, Nicolette decided she needed to go out on the dance floor and meet a guy. She was determined to meet someone, and I couldn't say that I thought her standards were too high tonight. As long as he was semi-attractive and had a dick, I thought she'd be okay.

She begged me to come down, but I declined and said I'd just sit here and watch our drinks. She made me promise I'd dance later, when we were done with them, and I agreed just so she'd go away. Keeping our drinks close, I watched as she went down to the dance floor and started dancing her little heart out. There weren't many people doing traditional dances; it was more nightclub-esque grinding and making out.

As I sat and watched her, I felt a tap on my shoulder, which caught my attention. I turned to see a man, maybe a few years older than me, with parted blond hair and blue eyes. He was standing alone, dressed in slacks and a button-up shirt with a few buttons loosened at the top.

"Here all by yourself?" he asked.

"Oh, no, I'm here with a friend. She's dancing," I said.

"And how come you aren't down there with her? A beautiful girl like you should be tearing up that dance floor," he said.

"Not really my thing. I just came to support her," I said.

"Mind if I take a seat?" he asked, as he pointed to the empty chair.

"Uh, sure, that'll be okay until she gets back," I said stupidly, as I didn't know what else to say.

I was never good at rejecting people. Hell, the last time my order got screwed up at a restaurant, I ate it just so I wouldn't have to deal with the confrontation. It just wasn't my thing.

"I'm Carter," he said, as he set down his beer.

"Hi, Carter, I'm Penny," I said.

"What a beautiful name. Short for Penelope, which originates from Greece," he said.

"Oh, yes, it does," I said, smiling.

"So, Penny, what do you do for a living?" he asked.

"I'm still in school. In my last semester, actually," I said.

"How exciting. I just got out last year. What are you studying?" Carter asked.

"I'm studying computer science," I said.

"Wow, that's amazing," he said, with relative shock. "There aren't nearly enough women in that industry as there should be. It's been male-dominated for the longest time, and it's about time women got in on it. I'm really glad to see that it's happening," he said.

"Yeah, it's been male-dominated since it began," I said, smiling, as I couldn't believe someone would say that.

I didn't think someone like Blake would say something so encouraging like that. He might think it, but maybe running a tech company could make you a little biased towards trends and how things have always been.

"I myself am in city planning. I guess it's sort of like computer science, with figuring out how things work and how to best place everything," he said.

"I can definitely see the comparison. Do you work for the city?" I asked.

"Sure do. It's a fun job, but it can be pretty stressful. I think the best part is seeing how your ideas are turned into realities all across the city. Like we're in stages to build a few new eco-friendly parks in the city that were my idea," he said.

"That's great. I think cities need more of those," I said, smiling.

I tried to be friendly and polite to Carter, even though I could sense what he was trying to do. After all, I was a girl alone in a club and he was obviously a single guy out to find a woman, whether it was just for the night or for all of his nights. I of course wasn't interested, as I was happy with Blake, but I suppose it was better to sit here and have a conversation with someone than to sit all alone and watch my best friend shake her ass.

"So, you said you're here with your friend?" he asked.

"Yeah, she's down there. She's my roommate, too. She wanted to go out and meet someone, I guess, so I said I'd come along," I replied.

"Don't you want to get out there and dance and meet someone?" he asked.

I didn't know if he was truly curious, or if he was trying to bait me into an answer he wanted. I wasn't going to give him one he wanted, though, and I was afraid of what he'd say.

"I'm already seeing someone," I said.

"Oh," he replied.

"I'm sorry. I think you're really nice!" I said.

"Well, I'm sorry for wasting your time," he said, with a saddened look on his face.

"You didn't waste my time! I like talking to you. You're a nice guy," I said.

"Yeah, a nice guy. Cause they always finish first," he said bitterly.

"Don't beat yourself up like that, Carter. There are tons of girls here who would love to go out with you," I said.

"Well, when you see one, let me know," he said, as he got up from the table.

"I hope you have a good time tonight," I said.

He politely said thanks and walked away and out of sight. I turned back around and saw Nicolette down below. I felt bad rejecting him like that, but what else was I supposed to do? Even if I weren't with Blake, I likely wouldn't be all that interested. He seemed nice enough, but I wasn't sure he was even my type. I guess you can't please everyone.

After about ten more minutes, Nicolette came upstairs and back to the table. She ordered a water, and was sweating a little. She took a sip of her Margarita and let out a huge sigh.

"What's wrong?" I asked.

"Nothing, just so thirsty. It gets so hot and humid down there," she said.

"Yeah, you look like you really worked up a sweat," I said.

"You should come down with me. It's a blast. One guy even asked for my number," she said.

"I don't have that problem, remember?" I asked.

"Can't ever go wrong with a little dancing. Once she gets me my water, I'm pulling you down there," Nicolette said.

Our waitress came back with a bottle of water and Nicolette handed her four dollars for it.

Outrageous, but I guess that's what you get for not stuffing one in your purse like me. After taking a few gulps and letting herself rest for a moment, she grabbed my hand and tried to get me to go with her. I refused, telling her it wasn't my thing, though she thoroughly insisted and wouldn't let it go until I went for at least ten minutes. If I didn't want to after that, she'd let me come back.

I went down with her, and we left our drinks behind and decided they weren't good enough anyway. We wiggled our way onto the dance floor and I felt a mass of sweaty, wet bodies rub up against me. I cringed, as any normal person would, before we got to a small area that was open and Nicolette started flailing around. *This* was her version of dancing?

"Come on," she said, grabbing my hands.

She swung them around before I started to move my body a little to satisfy her. The air was thick and I almost felt like I was swimming from the intense heat that ran across the dance floor. With beads of sweat forming across my brow, I swung my arms on my own, though I didn't enjoy it. I knew I should let go of my inhibitions and had a little fun, but it just wasn't for me.

Within a few minutes, two guys came up and tried to dance with us. Nicolette gladly danced with her guy, but mine, who kind of reminded me of Tyler, wasn't getting anything from me. I turned him away, telling Nicolette I wanted to leave. She rolled her eyes and told me I still had a few more minutes. I danced on my own, closer to her, as the guy who tried it with me moved onto another girl nearby.

I counted down the seconds before telling her I was going outside and going home. She was annoyed, but said okay and that she'd be out in a few to see how I was doing. I pushed my way through the crowd before walking up the stairs and towards the exit. I saw Carter on the way out, who flashed me a small smile. He was sitting there talking to an attractive girl. I felt happy for him, but not as happy as for myself the moment I walked outside and the cool air hit my face. I almost felt all the sweat freeze as my lungs were finally shocked with cold air and not that sweaty jungle air.

I took out my phone and unlocked it to see Blake had texted me fifteen minutes earlier.

"*How's dancing*?" he asked.

"*It sucks. I'm standing outside now because it was all just a little too much*," I replied.

"*I'm sorry to hear that. I'm still at work. We're entertaining another merger talk. It's boring*," he said.

"*At least you're not here*," I said.

"*I'd love to be dancing with you right now. I know you don't like to dance, but it'd be fun*," he said.

I felt my cheeks warm up a little as I thought about the two of us dancing. This wasn't the best environment for it, but I'd be down if it meant I was dancing with him. Maybe he could even teach me a few things.

"*I'd dance with you, just not here. We might catch something*," I said, jokingly.

"*Like dance fever?*" he replied.

"*That, and a possible skin infection*," I replied.

He sent back a smiley face and said he had to get

back to the meeting because he was getting annoyed looks. I said I'd talk to him later, and as I put my phone away, Nicolette came out, her hair slightly wet, her makeup starting to smudge and run from the humidity. It made me wonder what mine looked like.

"Are you leaving?" she asked.

"I don't know. This isn't that fun," I said.

"Oh come on, do it for me. I want at least another half hour, and then we can leave together. I promise," she said.

She looked at me with puppy dog eyes before I let out a sigh and agreed to another half hour. I told her this was all she'd get, and she agreed, but I had a feeling I'd have to drag her off the dance floor later.

I stood around the entire thirty minutes, as there wasn't a single stool open, before she came up, sweaty as can be, without a guy. I guess she'd paid attention to the time, which I couldn't have been more thrilled about. With her disappointed, we left the dance club and hailed a cab before getting in and telling the cabbie, a man this time, where we needed to go.

"I can't believe I didn't meet one stupid guy," Nicolette said, her arms crossed.

"You will next time. Use the app!" I said.

"I never find anyone on there. Maybe I'm just losing my edge," she said.

"No, don't say that. You're being ridiculous. You'll find a guy soon, I know it," I said.

Truthfully, I had no idea when she would or wouldn't find a guy, and not only because I wasn't psychic. Nicolette never seemed to do that great with long-term things. It wasn't that she was a bad girl, she wasn't, but she seemed to have commitment issues that I thought she never really wanted to admit to. I think she set herself up with too many expectations in terms of dating.

Instead of just finding a decent-looking guy who was nice to her and treated her right, she went for good-looking guys who treated her like shit. It was something that happened all too often with people I knew in general, and it was probably why Carter was referring to how nice guys never finish first, or whatever it was he said. I knew that wasn't true either, though. Just look at Blake and me. He truly was a good guy, even if he didn't necessarily show it at first. He was kind, caring, supportive, and just an overall good guy. He treated me well, and even though I hadn't been the best since we got back together, I liked to think I treated him great as well.

"Yeah, well, I hope it happens soon. You're lucky to have Blake. You seem happy," she said.

"I am happy, and you'll be happy too. Just work on yourself and stay single and happy, and that guy will come along when you least expect it. It happened to me, so I know it will happen to you. You're an amazing catch," I said.

"Thank you, Penny. You're a great friend," she said, as she looked at me with loving eyes. I didn't know if it was from the booze or not.

I scooted in closer and cozied up to her as girlfriends do when another is in distress, and we rode the rest of the way home before getting out of the cab and trudging up the five flights of stairs, which never really seemed to get any easier.

"Home sweet home," she said, as we walked through the front door.

I locked it behind us and tossed my purse in my room before kicking off my shoes, walking over to the couch, and rubbing my feet. It felt so damned good to get out of those confining shoes and finally let my toes breathe.

After sitting on the couch with Nicolette for an hour as we ate popcorn and peppermint patties, I finally decided it was time to get to sleep, as I could barely keep my eyes open between yawning. I quickly washed my face and half-assed brushing my teeth before shuffling into my room and checking my phone. Blake hadn't texted me since earlier, and I didn't bother to tell him goodnight, as I knew I wouldn't be awake to see the reply.

I got in my bed, pulled the covers up, and settled it as my mind wandered. I had that problem a lot at night, more so with insomnia, even when I was physically tired. I could feel like falling asleep, then get in bed and feel like staying awake, but mostly because my mind just wouldn't stop.

I thought about our upcoming trip, and the ramifications it was going to have on our relationship. It wasn't just going to be an average, everyday trip, not that I knew about those, considering how damned poor I was. This trip could signify a new step in our relationship that was bigger than anything I'd experienced with any man before. Hell, it could be the biggest step I'd ever have again, and I didn't want to mess it up.

What if Blake asked me to be his girlfriend,

formally, when we were on the trip? What if he asked me right after? What if this spring-boarded us into marriage one day? Okay, Penny, take a deep, long breath. It was just a business trip, after all. It wasn't like he asked me to the Virgin Islands or to Hawaii or Paris or something. It was a two-day business trip where he'd actually be doing business. It wasn't a code word for some kind of crazy thing. Still, though, I couldn't help but think he was going to try something on the trip.

After about twenty minutes, I checked my phone out of curiosity and saw he'd sent me a text saying goodnight and that he missed me. I replied, saying I was falling asleep, but I missed him as well and goodnight, before setting down my phone and rolling back under the covers. He always knew the right thing to say to calm me down, even if he wasn't here. I still couldn't believe I was so lucky to have him.

I calmed down, closed my eyes, and took a deep breath before I finally let myself beat my insomnia and start to fall asleep. This trip was going to be a life-changer.

CHAPTER TEN

Penelope

A few days later, school had provided nothing but misery for me. Homework, quizzes, tests, and more studying than I'd ever done in my life. My communications professor told us about a project that was going to be forty percent of our grade, and it would be due at the end of the semester in lieu of an actual final. I'd much rather have a final instead.

One good part of my school week was on Tuesdays, when we got to go into the computer lab and code new ideas. Our project, which was for my advanced coding class, was to build an app for a phone. We were given a random app topic, mine was a game, and we were to build something that would be launchable. It didn't need to be groundbreaking, since we weren't going to actually sell or publish them, but it had to be good enough to get a good grade. I'd made a jumping game where you jumped over these barrels that would come your way. It was still a work in progress, but it was a lot more fun than listening to a professor drone on.

I sat in the lab and typed away as I found a bug in my code that I couldn't seem to get past. Even though my professor was cool and was always around to help, I wanted to wait before asking him to come over. There was something about figuring it out on my own that was satisfying and worth the frustration. I knew I'd have to rely on a skill like this if I were to ever get a real job coding, and I couldn't ask somebody else to figure it out.

I scanned the code about five times before I finally caught the error. It was a wrong character. I was supposed to be a "1," but I accidentally typed "2" instead. I changed the problem and voila, it was working again. It was amazing to me how one little mistake like that could derail an entire operation. It was a good thing this was just a project and not something that would actually change lives.

The lab was kept a little dim, as much of the only light came from glowing computer screens. My class was rather small, maybe fifteen people, though I still thought it was rather large for this degree and course, especially at this school. My school wasn't huge, but it wasn't tiny either. There were probably better schools I could've gone to, but I wanted nothing more than to be in the city—this city, in particular. I was sure glad I made this decision.

After an hour and fifteen minutes, I came out of

the computer lab with slightly closed eyes as I tried to adjust to the light again. It was like being a bear coming out of hibernation. The computer lab was luckily my last class of the day, so I put on my jacket before walking outside and feeling the air, not as chilly as usual, as it tickled across my face.

I stood and waited for the bus before it finally came, late, and picked me and two other students up. The bus was relatively empty, at least for this time of day, so I found a seat up front and sat down before the driver took off like a madwoman, probably because of being late. She made her stops quickly and rolled through the ones with nobody there. She tried to do the same with mine, but I pulled the cord and she stopped to let me off, though it wasn't exactly at the bus stop.

As I walked down the street I saw Nicolette's car, which was odd because she still should've had another two hours before getting off work. I went into the apartment, checked the mail, of which there was a lot, and walked back up the stairs before opening the door and seeing her on the couch eating a salad.

"What are you doing home?" I asked.

"I had a dentist appointment after lunch and just decided to use some personal time and take the rest of the day off," she said.

"You can do that?" I asked.

"Of course. That's why it's *personal* time," she said.

I locked the door and tossed the mail on the counter before sorting through it. It mostly consisted of inserts and ads, though there was a power bill addressed to Nicolette, as well as a magazine renewal form for one of her girly magazines. I left them on the counter before going into my room and dropping off my backpack and purse and slipping into my pajama bottoms, which were much more comfortable than the tight-fitting jeans I'd been wearing.

"So, what are you doing tonight?" I asked, as I sat next to her on the couch.

"Oh, probably just this, why?" she asked.

"Just wondering. I have to do some more homework, but I might see what Blake is up to," I said.

"I saw him around the office today. Didn't say hi, but I saw him," she said.

"You should talk to him sometime," I said.

"Oh yeah, right, like I'm going to go talk to the CEO of the company I work for randomly and see how he's doing. I'd like to keep my job, thanks," she said.

"He isn't like that, Nic. And besides, he knows your name and that you work there. If he ever fired you, especially for talking to him, he knows I'd have his balls in a clamp," I said.

"True. I guess you fucking him gets me some job security," she said.

"We're more than just that," I said.

"So you guys are official?" she asked.

"Well, no, but—" I said.

"Get it official, girl. Then we'll talk," she said.

My trip with Blake was only three days away, and I had to say it had me a little nervous and a lot excited about whether he was finally going to ask me. It seemed odd that he would take me there for something as simple as making me his official girlfriend, but then again I never thought I'd be dating a billionaire at any point in my lifetime. Weird just wasn't totally in my vocabulary anymore.

He'd texted me earlier and said the private jet was scheduled and we would be leaving at ten in the morning. He said I should spend the night at his place so it would be easier, and I agreed, for more reasons than that. I couldn't believe he was taking me on a private plane, as I'd barely even been on a regular one before. What was the etiquette for it? Did we still have to go through security? Did we go to the regular airport and then to a special section there? I had no clue.

I texted Blake, telling him I missed him, and he replied thirty minutes later with the same, and told me he wasn't going to be able to see me until Thursday night when I came over. I guess they were finalizing a bunch of stuff that dealt with our trip and he wasn't going to be home much. Though admittedly I was a little disappointed, I knew he could have time away from me when I signed up for all this.

"So, when are you planning on telling him?" Nicolette asked.

"What?" I asked.

"You know, the whole using him thing or whatever," she said.

"I wasn't *using* him. I was just punishing him," I said.

"Still, when are you?" she asked.

"I don't know. I feel like I haven't even done anything towards him in a while. Things have just gone back to normal," I said.

"Well, you have to tell him," she said, looking at me.

"Why? I barely did anything," I said.

"Penny. You know you can't just go into a relationship with a guy and have that guilt hanging over your head. Especially not you. You're too good for that," she said.

"I'll tell him, I just don't know when. I don't want to rush it, you know? I want to wait to see if he actually asks me to be his girlfriend," I said.

"So you're going to wait until after that happens? You've got some big balls, girl," she said.

Maybe she was right, and I didn't admit to that often. What if waiting until *after* he asked me out was a bad idea? What if that really turned him off and he tossed me aside like I did to him? Shit, I don't know, but I really didn't want to come out with it, especially before or during this trip. I'd just wait until after. Yeah, that would be best and we could have a nice trip without any awkwardness or problems.

I got up off the couch before getting a cold bottle of water, going into my room, and shutting the door behind me. I sat on the edge of the bed, kicked off my socks, and looked out my little window at the people below. I sat and thought, mostly about what Nicolette had brought up, as my once fun-sounding trip started to sound a little scary and not so fun. What if I couldn't even have a good time when I was with him this weekend? What if I panicked the entire time about this and it ruined what could've been an awesomely amazing trip?

I had to forget about these problems, and forget about them I would. They'd be here when I got back, and I could deal with them, and him, then. For now, though, I was going to sit back, look over a textbook, and relax. I deserved it.

CHAPTER ELEVEN

Blake

I had been so busy with work lately that I almost forgot what day it was. Not only were we opening new offices in Seattle, but now the board wanted to buy yet *another* company to add to our cabinet of services. They said they wanted to get a bunch of proprietary technologies so we could venture out and do more things outside of the app. They said in order to keep ourselves relevant, we could even implement some of these things into the app.

The newest venture they wanted was a payment processing service, which actually wasn't a horrible idea. We'd implement it into our app for services like buying coins, and a premium-style membership, as well as rolling it out to the public as a payment service for anybody. You could send money to family, friends, businesses, and anything else you could think of. It was a great idea, but I was afraid it was running our resources rather thin.

We already had so many people working on so many different things that to do this we were going to have to hire more people and get more office space in addition to the ones we were already getting. That cost more money, time, and resources, and while we had all those things, they could be better spent somewhere else. When I started this business I never thought things would get so big and out of control. Some nights I've even lain in bed and wondered if it was worth it anymore. I could cash out my stock, get a shit-ton more money, and never have to work again a day in my life. I could move somewhere remote, maybe even somewhere tropical, and ask Penny to go with me and start a life somewhere new. We would travel the world, maybe have a few kids down the line, and it would all end with a happy story.

Even though that all sounded nice, magical really, I knew I really couldn't do it. I couldn't leave this company behind. Not only would the stock go down, but how would it look, especially after all this building, if the CEO and founder just up and left? It would be a news parade and I knew the business would ultimately suffer. There was nobody who had the level of decisiveness and need for control like I did. I treated this business as if it was my real child, and everybody knows a parent will do anything for his or her child. I was the same way with RandomMeetX.

I sat in my office as the night sky rolled in. I wanted nothing more than to be sitting in my media room with Penny, cuddled up on the plush leather sofa, as we sipped red wine and nibbled on dark chocolate. She'd fit perfectly in my arms and we'd laugh at all the stupidest stuff in the world. I would feel a warmth in my stomach as I heard her giggle.

I still couldn't believe the impact she was having on me. I never thought I could feel this strongly about a woman, especially at this stage in my life. Sure, I thought one day things would go great for me, and I'd meet an awesome girl who would change everything, but I expected a few more years before anything like that happened. Instead, I was blindsided as the awkward-looking girl who sat in my waiting room was destined to become so much more to me.

I'd decided I did want to make her my official girlfriend, if she was interested, though I was going to wait until after the trip with her this weekend. Even though it would be a little romantic, being in Seattle in the winter, I didn't feel like a business trip where I couldn't devote a ton of time to her was the best setting. What was I going to do, ask her and then run away to a meeting? I was better off forging a great time with her when we were together and then when we got back, having a special date where things could naturally fall into place.

I was fairly confident she'd say yes, but I wasn't sure how I'd react if for some reason she rejected the idea. I thought things were going great, and we hadn't had any problems to speak of, so I couldn't imagine she would say no, but you never know these days. Some people are just into casual things, while others want to meet the partner they're going to spend the rest of their days with. The two of us had never really talked about a real relationship either, so I might be stepping into a whole new world of shock and rejection, though I was praying it went well. I needed it to go well.

A stack of proposed files for the buyout sat in front of me. The board wanted me to go over them to see what I thought. I sat and piddled around on the computer playing a ninja game, which was sort of my guilty pleasure during my off-time. I wasn't technically on off-time, but I was the boss, so I could do whatever the hell I wanted half the time without any recourse. I wasn't exactly scared of a room full of old white men anyway.

After playing for about thirty minutes and needing to blink a few dozen times from keeping my eyes open too much, I picked up the first paper and put it in front of me. The amount of legal jargon and mumbo jumbo was almost overwhelming as I tried to keep my mind open and free of any distraction.

The first paper, which needed my signature, looked okay. I signed it in crisp black ink and put it to the side. As I picked up the second one, my phone buzzed, and I looked at it to see I had a text from Penny. I immediately put down my paper and unlocked my phone as I read her text and couldn't help but smile, which made me feel more like a fifteen-year-old girl than a corporate wizard.

"*Just thought I'd see how you're doing. I miss you and was thinking about you*," she said.

"*Just working my ass off looking over papers. I'd much rather be cuddling with you*," I said.

Penny had made me much more flirtatious, but in a different way. I'd always been flirty, but it was more in the "I'm devilishly handsome and I know you want to sleep with me" kind of way. Now it was more like the "I miss you and want to kiss you and cuddle you and wake up next to you" kind of way. Very different, at least in my mind.

"*Nobody is stopping you from coming over here and doing that*," she said, followed by a winking face.

I sent back a smiley face, as I told her I wanted to, but I couldn't, though we would be doing a ton of it Thursday night and especially on our trip. She said boo to me not coming over, and told me to get back to work so I didn't have to stay late on Thursday. I told her goodnight and put down my phone before picking back up that second sheet of paper and looking it over. I signed it even though I wasn't sure I fully understood it, but I knew the board and our legal team was never going to steer us wrong. I think they wanted me to read it more so I knew what was going on and not because they actually wanted my input or opinion.

I walked out of my office to get a drink. As I walked down the hall towards the break room I saw a few of the janitors cleaning and emptying trash bins. They nodded, I nodded, and I went inside where I got a cola, which was something I usually didn't drink all too often, and went back to my office. I closed my door, making sure to lock it, before taking a swig and going over the papers.

I ended up signing most of them, though I didn't have enough time to get through it all. There were too many papers and not enough minutes left in the rest of this day.

After about another hour, I put on my jacket, turned off my things, and put the files away in my safe before leaving my office and locking the door behind me. Janitorial staff didn't have access to my office without someone present, for fear that something could be stolen or copied for a rival. I knew it sounded a little crazy, but crazier things had happened in this industry. People killed for the tech secrets of tomorrow.

I rode down my private elevator to the parking garage, where a security officer standing nearby nodded as I came out. We had security on the perimeter twenty-four-seven to keep our building and floors secure. It was a small expense to make sure we didn't pay a huge one later on.

I got into my SUV and pulled out of the garage as I thought about stopping by Penny's place and picking her up. I decided against it because of the time, and went back to my apartment feeling a little empty. I had so much room here and I never even used it all. This place was better for a family of six instead of just me, and I barely even had Penny over enough to justify the room. I should just get a smaller place so I didn't feel so alone at night, but how could I beat the privacy and the car elevator? It was something I couldn't give up.

As the clock ticked on I washed my face, brushed my teeth, and looked in the mirror. Small bags started forming under my eyes, which were getting a little bloodshot. I needed some sleep, and I needed some *good* sleep for once. None of this waking up a ton shit would fly tonight.

I got into bed as I pulled the comforter up over me and snuggled in. It felt so good to be lying down, as I curled my toes underneath the cool sheets and felt myself in a cocoon of comfort that I never got anywhere besides this mattress.

As my eyes closed, all I could see was a vision of Penny in my mind. She was always the most soothing part of my day, and it was only fitting that she be present now as I drifted away to sleep.

CHAPTER TWELVE

Penelope

Thursday had finally come and I was more excited than I'd been in a while. I couldn't believe I was flying to Seattle tomorrow, and with my man no less. We were going to have a great hotel room, hopefully some amazing sex, and even do some sightseeing, which I was more than thrilled about.

I'd always seen so many amazing things in Seattle on the Internet and TV. The mountains, the charm, the overcast weather, and the Space Needle were so quintessentially Seattle that they couldn't be mixed up with anywhere else. We were going to go to the fish markets, stroll along the water, and hopefully see a view of the mountains from our hotel room, though I wasn't counting on that, no matter how expensive and luxurious it was. I didn't expect Blake to move mountains for me...literally.

My school day was going to be rather chill, though I did have a small quiz and a few pieces of homework to turn in. I did all of them last night, even though I slacked a little bit. I guess I'd been too excited to even care about school. My professors for my classes tomorrow were letting me turn in some things today, though, since I wasn't going to be here. That was nice.

I hadn't seen Blake in a few days, which felt like absolute torture. He sent me pictures and I sent him some of me, but it just wasn't the same as touching him and kissing him and feeling his fingers laced with mine. There wasn't a feeling that was even comparable to all that, and he was the only person in this world who made me feel those things.

I got off the bus and walked into class as my professor handed me the quiz to take. Other students, those who arrived earlier, were already taking it. I sat down, took off my jacket, and set down my backpack before taking out a mechanical pencil, a purple one with a worn down eraser, and looking over the test. My head started to spin, but since the time hadn't actually started yet because I was five minutes early, I tried to take a deep breath and figure it all out.

There was something about timed tests and quizzes that always got to me. It felt like a race, and I was better in situations where I had all the time in the world to figure problems out and come up with a solution. I guess being under pressure like that was my biggest weakness, and likely the reason I didn't go into a more fast-paced and panicked field like medicine. I was all right with deadlines, even if they were strict, but having a stopwatch timing me usually didn't go that great.

The tip of my pencil broke off and I brushed it to the floor before clicking the top a few times to get another small strand of lead to write with. I focused hard, too hard probably, and filled in bubble after bubble as other students around me, even ones who came in after me, got done with their work.

After fifteen or so minutes, I finished and blinked a few times to moisten my dry eyes. The professor came around and collected our quizzes before taking them back up front and setting them on his desk. I took notes for the rest of the period, half-assed notes really, as my mind was too preoccupied with the trip. I still had to do some laundry, get my bag packed, and make sure I didn't forget a thing, which was something I was known to do before any kind of overnight trip. Hell, the last time I went out of town I forgot my toothbrush, but not the toothpaste, and my face wash. Let's just say I wasn't always the best at packing.

My classes soon ended and like the other students, I quickly walked out of the building and got to the bus just as it was about to leave. I texted Blake and told him I was excited to see him later. He didn't reply right away, as he was likely in a meeting, but I couldn't help but look like a crazy woman smiling on the bus as I thought of this trip right around the corner. It was going to be grand.

I felt giddy and excited as Gustav pulled up in front of my apartment later that night. Blake was at home, cooking us a meal. Gustav walked around to the side and opened the door for me.

"So, are you excited for your trip?" Gustav asked, after getting back into the car.

"Beyond excited. Seattle looks like such a beautiful place," I said.

"You know, I don't think he's ever really taken a woman with him like this. At least on a business trip," Gustav said.

"Really?" I asked.

"Usually he takes his business so seriously that he doesn't want to risk embarrassment should they be at dinner with clients or whatnot and have someone misbehave or misrepresent him. It's really nice to see him trusting you like this," Gustav said.

Hearing this from Gustav just drilled into me more and more how great things were going between us. Gustav, though he wasn't exactly Blake's *friend* in a sense, knew him well and saw the many people coming in and out of his life. Was Blake that proud of our relationship? Did he feel comfortable enough with us, with me, that he thought I would never embarrass him or make him look stupid in front of important people? I had to admit I likely embarrassed him a little at that gala event, but I think he had that one coming.

"You know, when I drive him I catch him smiling a lot at his phone. Are you the reason for that?" Gustav asked, though I was sure he knew the answer already.

"I'd hope so. I know he makes me smile a lot," I said.

"You've really changed him, Penny, and in a good way. I'm glad he found you," Gustav said.

Filled with joy and a warm heart, I looked out the window as we drove to his building, as happy as could be. Gustav pulled into the garage and helped me out of the backseat before grabbing my bag and telling me he would take care of it. I walked over to the elevator and Blake quickly buzzed me up. I stepped inside before the doors closed and it started to heave upwards. After a short time, the doors opened and I saw Blake, in a suit, with a red rose in his hand and a smile on his face.

"Look at you," I said, smiling, as I walked off the elevator.

"I got this for you, my dear," he said, handing me the rose.

I sniffed it as I sort of rotated my foot on the ground in a girly way. I was smitten, and it was deadly obvious. Blake leaned in and kissed me, his hands firmly on my hips, and I felt a surge of electricity rush through my body. There was always something electric about kissing Blake, and now I was beginning to realize why. I think I was falling for him. I mean, why wouldn't I?

We got along great, we rarely fought, and whenever we were together it was like magic. I wasn't saying I was in love with him, I wasn't, at least not yet, but I definitely saw myself falling for him, hard. Who knows where we'd be in a month or two, especially if this sort of stuff kept up? It was scary to think about falling in love with someone like him, but I guess the heart wants what the heart wants. I only hoped he felt the same way about me, or at least something close to it.

"I made you dinner," he said, after pulling away from my lips.

"Did you make it, or did you heat it up?" I asked with a smile, teasing him.

"I made it! Well, someone else prepped it, but I used the stove *and* the oven," he said with pride.

"Well, it smells wonderful. I can't wait to try it," I said.

He held my hand and we walked over to the kitchen, where he took out a crystal vase and set my rose inside before filling it with water. I put my elbows on the edge of his countertop, looking at him with love-filled eyes, as he stirred the contents of his stainless steel pan.

He put some sauce on a spoon and took a taste before making a happy face and insisting I try it. I did, and was actually impressed with how good it was. I knew he didn't make it himself, but I didn't say anything about it.

"It all smells so good," I said, as Blake took the pans off the heat.

"Why don't you go sit down and I'll bring it to you. I want to pamper you," he said.

"Pamper me? Why?" I asked.

"No reason. Just want to," he replied, with a smile.

I walked over to the table, which was already set and featuring a bottle of wine sitting on ice in a bucket. He soon came over with our dishes and set them down.

"It's bruschetta chicken. You have the magnificently seasoned chicken in a balsamic vinegar and oil marinade over a bed of pasta that features some of that other sauce I just let you sample. We also have rustic garlic bread, a salad, and some dessert later, if you think you can handle it," he said.

"So, is this how it's always going to be? You making me meals?" I asked.

"I'm always down for taking care of you, but I think I'll let you try every now and again. It's somewhat tiring," he said, with a smile.

"Deal," I replied.

I cut into the chicken and grabbed a piece of it and some pasta before twirling it around and putting it in my mouth. The explosive flavors of the Italian spices took my taste buds by surprise as the tang of the balsamic vinegar fought against them. The chicken, which was as tender as could be, melted in my mouth. I savored every bite.

Blake looked at me with a smile as I ate my first bite before I enthusiastically told him how good it was. I thought he was a little suspicious of how nice I was being, but I truly meant every word I said to him. It was a meal that should have been in one of those gourmet five-star restaurants he liked to frequent.

"So, how did your day go?" he asked.

"Ugh, long. I had a quiz today and I'm sure I failed it," I said.

"I doubt that," he said.

"You don't even know. I was struggling to get through it. I needed life support," I said.

"Did you get through the entire thing?" he asked.

"Yeah," I replied.

"Then you did wonderfully. I bet you got a good grade," he said.

Blake was always so encouraging to me, even though most of the details of my life must have seemed so mundane to him. After all, he ran a multibillion-dollar tech company and I was just in a computer science program at a small school. I wasn't even close to being on the same playing field as he was.

"We'll see," I said, with a smile. "How did your day go?"

"It went well. I got done with all the paperwork I needed to do and submitted it to the board. The meeting tomorrow should go fairly smoothly, though you never know with these things. They could always bring in something from left field at the last moment. It's a good thing I won't be in there alone," he said.

"Are other people coming with us?" I asked, in an unsure tone.

"No, it'll be just us, but other people from the company, as well as our lawyers, will be present for the second deal we're doing. Preliminary stuff on the buyout of that other company. The new office space meeting should be fairly cut and dry, I'd imagine," he said.

"So, what am I doing during that time? Am I coming with you?" I asked.

"No, I think I'll just let you explore, if you'd like. You could always go shopping, or just sightseeing. I really wish I could be with you the entire time, but I'll get through my meetings as quickly as possible. I don't want to be there anyway," he said.

I was a little disappointed that I'd be set free alone, but I guess I was fine with it. It was better than sitting in some lobby somewhere while he was in his meetings. At least this way I could see the Space Needle or do something I wanted to do. I was sure I'd have a good time.

Blake and I soon finished dinner and he suggested we wait on dessert until later. The meal, which was starchy, sat in my stomach like a brick as Blake seemed to feel his in a similar manner. We kept our wine, though, and walked to the media room, where he turned on the television in lieu of a movie. He had a news ticker running across the top of the screen as he turned on a show where people tried to find houses in tropical locations. It was so beautiful seeing the turquoise-blue water and white sand beaches, and these people, who looked to be living a dream, were so unencumbered and relaxed.

"That looks so nice," I said.

"So you like tropical?" he asked.

"I think so. I've never really been to a tropical place, but I think it looks really nice to have the sand between your toes and to just lie on the beach without a care in the world," I said.

"Someone once said I should buy my own

island," Blake said.

"I'd do it," I said.

"Yeah?" he asked.

"Imagine going somewhere where nobody else was. Photographers, tourists, or no one else could bug you. You'd have so much privacy you wouldn't know what to do with yourself. You could still get one close enough to the mainland, but build your own little oasis on a smaller island nearby. It'd be paradise," I said.

"Maybe I'll have to keep that in mind, then. Would you ever come with me?" he asked.

"Would I? Yeah, I would! I'd love to," I said, with a smile.

He smiled back, before leaning in and kissing me softly. Our lips soon let go and I scooted in closer to him on the couch as he wrapped his arm around me and held me tightly. It was always so magical being here with him. I couldn't wait to get to Seattle.

We ended up skipping dessert later on, as the two of us were too tired and still too full to bother with it. We had an early flight, though Blake said it was okay if we were a little late. They weren't going to leave without us being there, which was a kind of service you definitely couldn't get on a commercial airline.

I unpacked a few things from my bag, things I was planning on keeping there, and Blake cleared out a drawer in the bathroom as well as one in his closet for me. I put in things I got at the store, like a new toothbrush, a toothbrush holder, toothpaste, and some face wash. I put some sleeping pants, some shirts, and some underwear in the drawer and felt a great sense of warmth come over me as I closed the drawers and made it official. It was a big step for me, for us, and I knew it meant bigger things were in the works.

As we got in bed I couldn't help but cuddle up to him. I put my head against him, listened to his heartbeat, and felt his fingers as they slowly ran through my hair and made me yawn. With my eyes half-open and drooping, I closed them all the way and drifted off to sleep.

CHAPTER THIRTEEN

Penelope

"Good morning, my little jetsetter," Blake said, as he got dressed next to the bed.

"Why didn't you wake me up?" I asked, rubbing my eyes.

"We still have some time. I thought I'd take a quick shower and get dressed before making us some breakfast," Blake said.

"That sounds nice," I said, before plopping my head back down against the pillow.

"Go get in the shower and I'll get started downstairs," Blake said.

I rolled out of bed and shuffled towards my bag before pulling out my clothes for the day and taking them into the bathroom with me. I set them down before turning on the shower, all fifty thousand sprayer heads, and walking inside once the area was nice and steamy. The water hit my body from all directions and I felt like I was in a human car wash. Every speck of dust and dirt on my body was quickly shot off. As one hit me right in the back I felt my muscles loosen and relax.

I washed off, trying to do so quickly, as I hadn't a clue how long we had before we needed to leave. I got dressed, dried my hair with my towel, and put on a little bit of light makeup before putting away my things and going downstairs. Blake just finished getting breakfast ready, as he set it on the counter and got out two plates.

"Nice shower?" he asked.

"Mm, yeah, I love that thing. All those sprayer heads are amazing," I said.

"It's probably the best investment I put into this place," he said.

We ate crepes with strawberries and bananas that melted decadently in my mouth. I couldn't believe the things I got to eat when I was with him, and it almost made me jealous that I couldn't eat this stuff all the time.

After we finished, Blake put the dishes in the sink and said that we needed to get going soon. We went upstairs, got our suitcases, and headed back downstairs before grabbing our jackets and heading down the elevator. Gustav was there, as always, and he put away our luggage before opening my door and helping me in. Blake got in on the other side and cozied up to me, and as Gustav got in the car, I saw him looking back at me in the mirror with a smile on his face. I was pretty sure this was the first time he'd actually been around us when we were together. I winked at him, thinking about our discussion earlier, and off we went.

I looked over at Blake as I held his hand and got closer to him. Traffic was horrendous, and Blake was looking at his phone, checking his email and the news, which was probably what he did all the time when Gustav drove him. I kept my mouth shut, opting to not say anything, as I just enjoyed the view. It was peaceful just looking out of the window.

We pulled into a private airport, which was wildly different from any commercial one I'd ever been to. It was small, a regional place, and there were no jumbo jets anywhere in sight. There were only private planes for people like Blake and tiny little planes with a propeller on the front. We pulled up to the plane, which was sitting there with the steps down, and the pilots came off the plane with the flight attendant.

Gustav opened our doors and helped us out before we said goodbye and he took out our luggage for the crew to handle. We walked up to the pilots, who Blake must've used before, because he smiled and shook their hands while asking how their families were. I introduced myself, and the pilots said we were leaving in about fifteen minutes. The flight attendant, Paige, welcomed us and asked if we'd like any drinks. I passed, but Blake said water would be fine. We walked up the steps and into the plane.

The seats, which were wrapped in a light tan leather, must have been softer than the clouds they flew through, and the interior, which was a glazed wood, looked as if it had been polished a thousand and one times. I sank into my seat as I sat down and felt as if I were weightless. I knew I could easily fall asleep in this, but it was only a two-hour flight. Besides, I'd just had a full night's sleep in the most luxurious bed known to mankind.

Paige brought Blake his water, and the pilots soon came back onto the plane and it was locked up. They went into the cockpit, making sure everything was good, before announcing over the intercom that we were heading out. The plane pulled out before getting onto the runway and I felt my stomach tumble a bit. I wasn't great on planes, and I really hadn't been on them all too often during my lifetime. I think it had to do more with the takeoff than anything else. I'd rather have my feet firmly on the ground than be thirty thousand feet or however high this thing went up in the air.

We turned around and sat at the end of the runway. I gripped the wooden armrests with all my might. My hands, which were turning a little white from gripping so hard, wouldn't let go of this seat even if the plane ripped in half. Blake, who was sitting across from me, didn't even notice as he read a magazine like nothing was bothering him. How was he so calm? I guess flying a lot makes you a little more used to what's going on around you. I wasn't so lucky.

I didn't say anything to him as the engines began to roar and our little jet started to accelerate at what felt like the speed of sound. I felt my stomach drop as

I closed my eyes and tried to take deep, steady breaths so I wouldn't get too anxious. I felt the front wheels lift off the ground before the back ones did the same, and we were airborne. My ears popped as I opened my jaw to try to fix the problem, but to no avail. As we turned a little, my stomach turned even more, and I felt something against my knee. I opened my eyes to see Blake, looking concerned, his hand on my knee.

"It's okay. I know you're scared, but we're safe," he said.

And suddenly, I felt a little calmer. My hands softened on the armrests and I began to get feeling back in them. Blake kept his eyes locked on mine, which admittedly helped a lot, as I couldn't be tempted to look out the window.

"Are you better?" he asked.

"Yeah, a little," I said.

"Take a sip," he said, before taking the cap off his bottle of water and handing it to me.

I took a big sip, a few big ones, actually, before handing it back and taking a deep breath. As the plane stabilized in the air, I felt normal, as I knew that the worst part was over. There was something about feeling like I was being ejected thousands of feet into the air that never sat well with me and likely never would.

Blake handed me a shopping magazine and told me to keep myself occupied so I'd be okay. I accepted his advice and went through the magazine, looking at outlandish toys and gadgets that I knew were never necessary, yet most people desired them. There was something about a two-in-one potato peeler and back scratcher with a laser on it that just screamed, "I need that."

Paige took care of all our needs, as she was always a moment away in the back of the plane. I didn't know what she did back there, but I bet she was incredibly glad to be doing it here and not on a regular aircraft. At least she didn't have a lot of snotty passengers causing her grief.

I set down the magazine and took a small catnap, as the change in pressure and oxygen seemed to make me a little tired. I put my hands in my lap, put the back of my head against the pillow cloud of leather, and dozed off for a little bit longer than I'd anticipated.

When I awoke, the wheels were skidding against the runway and we'd landed in Seattle. My eyes jolted open, the sound scaring me awake, as Blake smiled and told me we were finally here. I wiped my eyes, took a sip of water, and felt calm again as I looked outside and saw we were slowly going towards our destination. I'd successfully gotten through a two-hour flight without any problems, and I couldn't have been happier.

A car waited outside as Blake shook the pilots' hands and said goodbye to Paige. The driver, who sadly wasn't Gustav, welcomed us as our luggage was taken off the plane and set inside the SUV's trunk. We got in the back, cozied up together like on our earlier car ride, and the driver got back in and took us towards our hotel.

"So, where are we staying?" I asked.

"The Four Seasons, of course," Blake said with a

smile, as if I should've known.

As we left the airport and were soon in the streets of Seattle, I couldn't have been more thrilled. I looked out my window like a child and gazed in awe at the beautiful streets and buildings. It was all so…magical. San Francisco had almost corrupted me, and even though it was a beautifully winding city, it was nothing compared to Seattle. I almost wanted to look for tech jobs up here, where I knew there would be a lot, but that meant leaving Blake and Nicolette, which wasn't an option in the slightest.

Our car pulled up to the Four Seasons as a doorman, who was a bit older, opened my door and held my hand as I got out of the car. Blake came around the other side, as another doorman opened his door, and buttoned his suit jacket as we stood outside the hotel. The building, which was incredibly modern, screamed elegance. The lines outside were sharp and long as the building itself looked like something out of an art exhibit. I'd seen nice places like this before in magazines and on TV, but never in person. I couldn't believe I was going to stay here.

"Good morning, Mr. Hunter. My name is Jack Writhe, and I'm the general manager of the Four Seasons Seattle. On behalf of our entire company, I'd like to formally welcome you for the night," Jack said, as he shook our hands.

"It's nice to meet you, Jack. I know we're a little early, but I hope that's okay," Blake said.

"That's more than fine. We here at the Four Seasons pride ourselves on efficiency and professionalism. We've taken the liberty of checking you into your room early, and I'd love to personally escort you there as our bellhops take care of your bags. We have you booked in our Presidential Suite, and if you'd follow me, I'll take you there," Jack, said.

I looked at Blake with a smile as Jack led us towards the room. I couldn't believe I was staying in the Presidential Suite. It all sounded so...presidential! I'd seen things in movies about these types of rooms, but I always thought they were made up just for the movies. I didn't actually think they had these grand rooms available for regular people to stay in. Well, I guess Blake wasn't a regular person, the more I thought about it.

The glitzy lobby, which felt as grand as that in the White House, shimmered in my eyes as we walked towards the elevators. Jack told us all about Seattle in the interim, as well as things to do if we were interested, and said that we had a full-time concierge available twenty-four-seven should we need anything at all. We could want a single stick of gum and they'd get it and bring it to us within minutes.

As we stood in front of the room, which featured two massive doors, I was a little nervous and excited. Jack opened the doors, which swung effortlessly, and revealed a beautiful view of the water. I walked in and my jaw dropped as I looked over Elliott Bay. The water was breathtaking as the massive and incredibly clean windows framed the most beautiful aspects of Seattle like they were in a painting. Birds flew overhead and I swore I saw a whale breaching far in the distance, though I was likely imagining it. I couldn't believe I was here.

"The suite, which is just short of 2,500 square feet, features a king-sized bedroom, a marble bath, and also a guest bath with a shower, should you have any visitors. You will find all of your modern amenities and more, and you will have full access to our spa and facilities, should you wish. There are multiple telephones around the suite, should you feel the need to use them. We are always available for you, and will fix any problem you may have. I am going to give you the key, and please, let me know if there are *any* problems," Jack said, before handing Blake and I room keys.

"Thank you for your time, Jack. I greatly appreciate it. We'll let you know if we need anything," Blake said, before shaking Jack's hand.

He nodded and walked out the doors just as two bellhops were placing our luggage inside the room. They left, closing the doors behind them. I turned back around and looked out at the view.

"Amazing, isn't it?" Blake asked.

"Yeah, I read about it before in a travel article. I can't believe I'm here looking at it, though, and from up here!" I said.

"Tenth floor is nice. It's not as high as some places in San Fran, but there aren't a ton of skyscrapers here. I like it. You have Elliott Bay and Puget Sound right there in front of you, like it's there only for your enjoyment. This room isn't bad, either," Blake said.

"*Room*?" I asked. "This is more like a house. Hell, it's *bigger* than most houses."

"It's amazing what money can buy. It was a

bargain for the night," he said.

"I don't think your idea of a bargain is the same as mine," I said.

"Yeah, probably not," he said, smiling.

"When's your first meeting?" I asked.

"Soon. I have about twenty minutes to just hang out, though, if you'd like to," he said.

"Of course. There's nothing I love more than spending time with you," I said.

We sat down on the sectional couch and looked out over the bay as small boats whizzed by. I looked at him, as his gaze was focused outside and not on me. We were finally here, and that meant more than one thing. I was going to have to tell him about what I did soon, and I wasn't sure how he was going to take it. Being here with him almost made it seem more real, and I knew I wasn't going to be able to hide from it for much longer. What if I had to tell him here? What if he asked me to be his girlfriend tonight or tomorrow? I had to tell him before that happened.

"I should get going. I got a notification that my car is here," Blake said.

"Will I see you soon?" I asked.

"Very soon. Let me know if you decide to go out and do anything. Please feel free to do so. Use this if you want to get yourself something or see something," Blake said, handing me a credit card.

"Thank you," I said.

"You're welcome," he said, before kissing me.

I walked him to the door before closing it and going back to my spot on the couch. I didn't know if it was the room, the view, or being way up here, but something about being here was making me think a lot. How was I going to go about this? How was I going to make it through? I guess all I could do was try, and try I would. I just hoped it didn't blow up in my face.

CHAPTER FOURTEEN

Blake

but I suppose she knew the nature of this trip and that I'd have to go and conduct business. It was still a little crazy that she was even here with me. I never would've thought of bringing a girl I was seeing or an ex-girlfriend with me on a trip before, but there was something about her that made me know it was okay. I knew she wouldn't cause any problems or make me regret it, and I wanted nothing more than to give her a trip she so very much deserved. She'd worked so hard in her life and seemingly gotten so little in return. She was barely scraping by when I came along, and although our arrangement wasn't what it once was, I knew it was on to bigger and better things.

I'd planned something for us that I knew she was

going to love. The one thing she really wanted to see, the Space Needle, was going to let us into their restaurant with an accelerated reservation so that we could have a special night together. I'd reserved a table, though I opted not to rent out the entire place, as I wanted to give other couples a chance at romance on this night. The weather forecast was fairly clear, and at around five hundred feet in the air, we'd dine in the clouds as we looked over the city.

I knew it was dangerous to not tell her, for fear that she would go there on her own today and see the view without me, but I felt like it was too big of a surprise to tell. I wanted to tell her we were going to dinner, have her get dressed, and then just take her there without telling her. I knew it was something she'd never forget.

I sat in the meeting as paper after paper was presented. We were renting temporary spaces, as we were still in negotiations to demolish a few old vacant buildings and build a new facility just for our company. The building our San Francisco branch was in obviously wasn't just for us, as it was a skyscraper, but this lovely little place would be just RandomMeetX and its subsidiaries, which were growing by the minute.

As I sat in my executive leather chair, I looked out a nearby window and towards the bay as I wondered if Penny was still on that couch, looking over it as well, and if she missed me as much as I missed her. All I wanted to do was expedite this meeting, but it seemed to go at a snail's pace as more amendments were added to the agreement. The city was giving us trouble about building this new facility. You'd think they'd want more business and jobs in their city, but I guess that wasn't how Seattle rolled.

As the negotiations came to an end six hours later, I was far too happy to shake everyone's hands and call it a day. I had a meeting tomorrow morning, but I still had some of the day to give to Penny and make her entire trip. Our plane wasn't going to leave until around seven tomorrow night, so I knew we'd be able to have unencumbered fun in this beautiful city.

As I walked out and got into my car, I pulled out my phone to let Penny know I was coming back to the hotel. She texted back, saying she was there, and that she couldn't wait to see me. I smiled, like I always did when I talked to her, and put my phone away as we sat in a little traffic that was anything but joyful.

When we pulled up to the hotel, my door was opened and I nodded to the doorman as I buttoned my suit jacket and briskly walked towards the elevators. Staff said hello to me along the way, even calling me by name, which was something that seemed to happen whenever I visited a hotel. I guess they told their employees somebody important was coming and made them be on their best behavior.

I slid my key card in the door and saw the green light before opening it. Penny was on the couch with a bottle of wine on some ice. With two glasses in her hands, she clanked them together before smiling as the soft glow of the falling sun gleamed on her supple red cheeks. I was smitten as I looked at her smile, causing me to smile too, before I walked towards her and took a glass from her hand. I poured the wine into our glasses and we toasted to a great vacation. We both took a sip from our glasses as we kept our eyes on one another.

After taking a few sips I set my glass down, and Penny did the same. I wrapped my arm around her shoulders and she cuddled up to me like she always did. As I ran my fingers through her hair, we looked out over the bay. The sun glowed like a fiery mass, the red and yellow colors like paint cast over the twinkling water.

I might not have been in a tropical setting, but I was in paradise. As I held this woman in my arms, I knew I would never let her go.

CHAPTER FIFTEEN

Penelope

Blake told me we were going to dinner somewhere I'd really like and to wear something nice. He said it was a classier place, so to wear something sexy, but also I guess a little conservative. That was all I really ever wore, so it wasn't a problem at all.

I asked him about three times where we were going, but every time he only told me it was a surprise. I didn't get to know what type of food they served, where in town they were, or even a single letter of their name. Maybe it was a small way he could exert control like he used to, or maybe he was just incredibly excited to take me.

I wore a black dress with small bits of glitter strewn throughout. The top had thick straps and showed no real cleavage. This was about as conservative as it got with a nice dress. As he saw me come out of the room, he smiled and told me how beautiful I looked.

"So, when are our reservations for?" I asked, as I put on my shoes.

"Twenty minutes from now or so. We should get going. I got an alert that our car is waiting downstairs," he said.

"Is this place far away?" I asked.

"It's an okay distance," he said.

I grumbled internally as I wished I would've been able to get *something* out of him. I thought he'd do well if he were ever captured and tortured for information. He'd never give anything up.

As we got out to the car, our driver smiled and opened the door for us as we scooted in and cozied up to one another. The doorman waved goodbye as we pulled out and began our journey. When we passed or came close to restaurants I looked at them and wondered if each one was it. We passed a lot of Asian places, but the driver just kept going, and Blake never said anything to try to stop him. I guess it was really that good.

After a few minutes, I looked out my window and got a few passing views of the Space Needle. It glowed in the dark like a giant light attracting bugs, and I saw people on the street taking pictures and gazing up at it. I still wanted to see it tomorrow, and Blake did say he had a lot of time open, so hopefully I'd get to go up.

Our driver pulled up on the side of the street near the Space Needle and I looked around for places where we could have reservations. I looked back at Blake, who was smiling, as the driver got out of the car and came around to my side.

"Where are we eating?" I asked, confused.

"Here," he said.

"On the ground?" I asked.

"No, up there," he said, as he pointed up towards the top of the Space Needle.

The driver opened the door and as I got out, I looked all the way up towards the giant needle and had my mouth open as I wondered how. How were we going to eat up there? How were we going to get up there to eat? Were we going to eat on top of the needle itself?

"How?"

"There's a restaurant up there. It turns and gives a panoramic of the city and the bay. I thought you'd enjoy it. Would you still like to go?" he asked.

"Are you kidding me? Of course I do! Let's go," I said, grabbing his hand and dragging him with me.

We rode an elevator up towards the restaurant. I couldn't have been giddier. I kissed him as we went up, slowly, as the butterflies he gave me couldn't have been even a tiny bit more intense. To think he did this for me, and thought of something I *really* wanted to do and did it, showed me that he was something else. It also made me nervous that he did it for a reason, though. What if he asked the question tonight? What if, on top of the Space Needle, I had to tell him what really happened and be honest with him? It definitely wouldn't create a great lasting memory for my first time here, but it would sure leave one.

As the elevator doors opened and the sweeping circular room greeted us, a hostess welcomed us before asking if we'd made reservations. Blake said his name, and as always, she perked up and treated us like royalty. One good thing about being with him was that nobody gave us bad service. It was almost like they knew their ass was on the line if they ignored us or were rude. It almost made going out more fun.

"Please, if you'd follow me, I'll escort you to your table," the girl said.

We walked behind her through the room, which was filled with the softened chatter of other patrons. I didn't see any children, and not everybody was dressed formally, but I couldn't have cared less. I just wanted to be here, and here I was.

"This is the best table in the house," she said, as she took a gold metal reserved sign from the table.

"Thank you so much," Blake said.

"You're most welcome. Your server will be with you shortly, and I hope you have a very enjoyable meal," she said, smiling, before walking away.

I couldn't even be bothered to look at the menu as I stared out the windows. We were at the start of a new rotation, with our current view showing the bay and surrounding area. It was like something I'd see in some big-budget Hollywood romance movie, but I was the one living it. This was *my* reality.

"Hello, my name is Bertram, and I'll be your waiter for this evening. How are you folks doing tonight?" Bertram asked, as he looked back and forth at us.

"Very well, thank you. And yourself?" Blake asked.

"I'm great, thank you so much for asking. Is this your first time here at SkyCity Restaurant?" Bertram asked.

"It is. It's a beautiful place—and view!" Blake said.

"Yes, isn't it magnificent? If you haven't noticed, we're rotating as the viewing platform moves. While your view right now won't stay static, it will be back shortly. May I start you two off with a drink, or perhaps an appetizer?" Bertram asked.

"Yes, please bring us a bottle of your finest red. Price isn't an issue. What would you recommend for an appetizer?" Blake asked.

"Our beef carpaccio is a great seller, and will pair nicely with the wine. Does that sound appetizing?" Bertram asked.

"Yes, I believe it does," Blake said.

"Great! I'll get that order in and fetch your wine. Thank you," Bertram said, before walking away.

"I hope it's okay I ordered that," Blake said.

"It's fine. It sounds delicious," I said, before looking back out over the city.

Bertram came back with the wine, letting Blake and me sample it. We both loved it, and that must've made Bertram happy, as he smiled and poured us each a glass before leaving the bottle with us. Our appetizer soon came, and as I saw the beef laid out in front of me, my mouth began to water.

I took a bite and the meat melted in my mouth like it was made of butter. I closed my eyes a little, letting out a tiny moan. Blake was looking at me when I opened my eyes. I gave him a slightly embarrassed look, as I wondered how many people around me heard me do a sex moan inside a restaurant. It wasn't my fault this was so damned good.

"How are you enjoying the dish?" Bertram asked, five minutes later.

"It's great," I said.

"I'm so glad you're liking it. Have you had a chance to look over the menu, or would you like more time?" Bertram asked.

"I think we're ready," Blake said.

"Great. What can I get for you?" Bertram asked.

"I'll have the prime Angus tenderloin," Blake said, closing his menu.

"And for yourself?" Bertram asked, as he looked at me.

"I'll have the same thing," I said, as I closed my menu.

"Excellent. If you don't mind me asking, are we celebrating anything special tonight?" Bertram asked.

I looked at Blake as I waited for him to answer. He took a few seconds, not saying a word, and my anxiety intensified as I waited. Well, Blake, are we? I thought.

"Actually, we are," Blake said, as he smiled at me.

I felt my stomach drop as I wondered if this was it. Was he going to ask me to be his girlfriend? No, he couldn't, at least not in front of the waiter. He seemed like a nice man and everything, but I didn't want him standing in front of us as Blake said this to me. I also didn't want him here when I had to stop Blake and tell him my secret.

"It's her first time in Seattle and I thought we'd come here to celebrate that. She's wanted to come to the Needle for quite some time," Blake said.

"Well, I'm very happy you decided to dine with us and get to see our entire city from so high up. We certainly welcome you and hope you'll see us again in the future," Bertram said.

"Thank you. I know I'll be back," I said, with a friendly smile.

Underneath my smile was a whole bunch of confusion and a hint of relief. Sure, I wanted to wait to tell Blake, and sure, I didn't want to cause a scene here, but at the same time I did want him to say something and look me in the eyes before asking me to be his. Maybe I was being a stereotypical girl, but I kind of wanted him to not be embarrassed and ask me in front of the world.

Blake and I talked about his business deal as well as just everyday topics as we waited for our food. He held my hand on top of the table, which gave me butterflies, as he kept showing me other sides to him that ranged from sweet to downright sexy. I couldn't wait to see what happened when we got back to the hotel tonight.

Bertram brought our food and made sure we were all set before we dug in. The steak was even more tender than our appetizer, as I could barely chew it before it melted away in my mouth. How they got this meat to act this way I'd never know, but I certainly was not complaining.

"How is yours?" Blake asked, as he cut effortlessly into his.

"Amazing, and yours?" I asked.

"The same. I live for fine dining, if you couldn't tell," he said.

"Oh, I've definitely noticed. You seem to always know the best places to go and the best things to get," I said.

"What can I say? I have great recommendations from people. I've also had Grace look up and research places for me to go," he said, with a chuckle.

"So she's a good secretary?" I asked.

"Yeah, much better than the last," he said.

"Why?" I asked.

"She wasn't exactly the most truthful person in the world. She held back some very important information from me that I can't disclose, and it made me furious. I know it seems odd given what happened between us, but I can't stand lying," he said.

"It's okay. I understand. It was different," I said nervously.

"I just don't like to keep liars in my life. I only like people I can trust, like you. It makes me feel more secure. I feel like so many people have tried to use me, and it's so hard to find those genuine people who don't try to use me for my things. I try not to keep those people around," he said, before taking another bite.

I could tell that even though he was saying these things, he wasn't directing them towards me. He wasn't being sarcastic or trying to bait me into admitting anything; he was just venting. The worst part about it, though, was that I was doing exactly what he hated. What if he got rid of me when I finally told him? It was making me wonder if this was a secret I should just take to the grave.

I didn't say anything, as I figured being quiet was likely my best course of action. This dinner and this night were too great to mess up just because I wanted to talk. Besides, the view outside did enough talking for the both of us. It was still as breathtaking now as it was when we first came in, and I'd been looking at it for most of that time.

We finished our dinner and sat sipping our wine as the chef brought us some gourmet artisanal chocolates that were made locally. We chatted with him for a few minutes and told him how delicious his food was. Blake offered many words of praise, which I thought meant a lot to the chef, as he seemed genuinely appreciative.

The chocolates were soon gone and only droplets were left in our wine glasses. Blake hadn't asked me the question yet, and I figured it wasn't going to happen tonight—at least not here. That was okay, though. I guess it gave me a little more time.

When the restaurant began to close, we left last. We got onto the elevator and rode down alone to our waiting car, which was parked right out front. A small drizzle came down as we hurried in and shut the doors behind us.

The asphalt and sidewalks were shimmering as the light rain coated them underneath the city lights. I looked back up one more time at the Space Needle and said goodbye to the magical place that I never wanted to leave. Why couldn't I just move in above the restaurant? I'd be okay with that. I really didn't even need much room!

As we walked into our room later, I was more than excited to kick off my shoes, walk over to the couch, and fall down onto it. It felt good to just be back and relax. Blake sat next to me, asking me to come over, and I fell right into his strong arms. I put my legs in his lap, my head on his shoulder, and wrapped my arms around his torso as we looked out at the ships in the bay. Neither one of us said a word, not even a grunt, but in some ways, we were saying so much.

I awoke the next morning to breakfast in bed as Blake brought a tray over to me.

"Good morning, beautiful," he said.

"Good morning, yourself," I said, as I yawned and wiped my eyes.

"I have to get to my meeting in a minute, but it shouldn't take too long. I'll hopefully be back before eleven. In the meantime, eat, shower, and I'll see you soon," he said, before leaning in and giving me a long kiss.

I gladly kissed him back before he left. There were Belgian waffles, strawberries, scrambled eggs, and buttered toast. It all smelled so good. A room service cart to the side held even more delights in case I was still hungry.

It was a little annoying not being able to cuddle in bed with Blake this morning or take a shower together in this wonderful bathroom, but I guess I knew this was a business trip when I agreed to go. He'd told me multiple times about his meetings, and I just needed to deal with it.

I ate my food slowly as I looked out the bedroom window and gazed in awe at the mountains in the distance. It was a clear enough day that I could see them, and they held a sort of trance over me. I could barely look away. Maybe next time I came I could ask Blake if we could take a plane or helicopter up to see them. That would be very neat and incredibly romantic—at least to me.

I set my tray aside on the room service cart when I was done as I burped and wiped my mouth. I opened my suitcase, which sat on a stand, and dug through my clothes before finding a tight-fitting flannel shirt, a white cami, and some dark wash jeans I thought would look cute and very Seattle-y. I guess it was my take on modern grunge, and where better to wear that than Seattle?

The shower, while not as opulent as Blake's, had multiple jet heads that sprayed me all over. I turned up the heat, and as the glass doors got foggy I was sure I'd come out looking like a prune. The toiletries, which were premium and better than my own stuff at home, lathered luxuriously, and the towels, which felt as soft as fur, wicked away all the moisture from my body as I got done. I wrapped the white towel around myself, walked out of the shower, and got ready for the day, which didn't involve much. I left most of my makeup off like I normally did and did my hair simply before I got dressed and checked myself over.

I got my phone, took a full-length mirror pic, and sent it to Blake, who within five minutes told me I looked beautiful and that he was close to leaving the meeting. I smiled at both parts of his text and put my phone away before walking out into the living room and seeing the view of the bay once more. I hadn't a clue whether we were going to be coming back here later tonight, since our flight wasn't too far away, and I didn't want to miss out. I took my phone back out, opened my camera, and took a few pictures for Nicolette, more to make her jealous than anything.

The city of Seattle was enchanting as Blake and I walked hand in hand down its streets. It was so alternative, so progressive, and more modern than I could've ever dreamed of. I knew San Francisco was many of these things as well, but I think you notice it even more when you're out of your home element. I'd gotten so used to San Francisco that I almost didn't notice things as I walked past them anymore. Here, though, everything was new and exciting, like the people with tattoos, flannel shirts, and even sporty looking moms pushing their strollers as they jogged down the street. There was always something to look at.

"Look at that!" I said, as we passed a small

chocolate shop.

The sidewalks were busy on this early Saturday afternoon, but nobody seemed to recognize Blake in the slightest. It was always nice when we could just walk around together and not be bothered. I knew he wasn't a celebrity by any means, but he might as well have been, with the way some people reacted around him. You'd think they were around a living god or something.

We walked inside a small café and were gladly welcomed as the aroma of freshly brewed coffee beans jolted my senses. Plates of perfectly pressed paninis and sandwiches whizzed by me towards their tables. The menu, which was a board hanging above the coffee roasters, was jam-packed, featuring everything you could think of. Feeling a bit overwhelmed, I picked the first thing I saw that looked good.

"May I take your order?" a girl behind the register asked.

"I'll have the turkey and cranberry panini," I said.

"Okay, what would you like for a side? We have homemade chips, a baguette, a side salad, or a fruit cocktail," she said.

"I'll have…the baguette," I said, after a second of thinking.

"Okay, and for you?" she asked, as she looked over at Blake.

"I'll have the Grunge, with some chips. Also two fountain drinks, please," Blake said, as he took out his wallet.

He paid after she repeated our order and gave us

our drinks. We walked over to the drink station, which featured flavored teas and waters, as well as several sodas. I picked a diet soda, which was usually what I got when I drank soda, even though I knew it wasn't the best for me. I was on vacation for a little while longer, though, so I guess I could treat myself.

We sat down at a table with our number displayed on the edge. I took a sip of my drink, which I splashed with a lime, and we played footsie with one another a little.

"So, did you enjoy the trip?" he asked.

"It's not over," I said.

"Well, you know what I mean," he said.

"Yeah, I loved it. The dinner last night was amazing," I said, with a smile.

"I knew you'd like it. I hated keeping it from you because I was so excited to tell you, but your face was worth the anguish of waiting," he said.

"I hate that we have to go. I like being out on a trip, alone, with you," I said.

"We could come back someday," he said.

"That'd be nice, but I also want to try that whole tropical thing you talked about," I said.

"How about we do that next and *then* come back here," he said, with a smile.

"Sounds like a date," I replied.

"Here you two go. Is there anything else I can get for you?" a woman asked, as she brought our food to our table.

"No, I believe that's it," Blake said.

"Awesome. Enjoy!" she said, before walking away.

"Yours is insane," I said, as I looked at his sandwich.

It was turkey, ham, bacon, a mound of melted cheese, some sauces, onions, lettuce, and mushrooms that were all slopped together and oozing. I guess the name *the Grunge* was a perfect name for something like this. Even though it seemed incredibly fattening, I still thought it looked good. How he was going to keep his abs after eating that, though, was beyond me.

My sandwich, which was nice and light, filled me up just the right amount. The baguette, which I smothered in locally-sourced whipped butter, had the right amount of snap and toughness. Blake downed all of his, which didn't really surprise me, before pushing his plate forward, covering his mouth, and burping a little off to the side.

"That's all you got? Pussy," I said.

"What?" he asked.

"That burp. Children do better than that," I said.

"Yeah?" he asked.

"Yup," I replied.

He looked at me, his chin going down a little, before he belted out a belch that shook the table and caused everyone around to look at him. Looking a little embarrassed, he put his hand up, as if he were saying sorry. I smiled. I loved that he broke out of the macho shell he usually tried to give off.

"Better," I said.

"Best," he replied.

I smiled before taking a sip of my diet soda and looking out the window as some clouds were starting to roll in overhead. Blake received a phone call from the pilots, saying we had to push forward our flight time and they were wondering if we could be there in an hour or less. I said that was fine, as I didn't want to be stranded here, and we quickly walked back to the hotel and got our things together.

It was a little disappointing not having more time with him in the city, but with a massive storm on its way, I didn't want to be stuck here, and I knew he didn't either. We had work and school, and I didn't pack any more clothes besides the ones from yesterday and the ones I had on now. Being trapped wouldn't have been very fun.

As we got to the airport, the pilots insisted we quickly get on so we could taxi and take off. We did so, and ran up the stairs before getting in our seats and asking for some water from the flight attendant, the same one from before. She brought them to us, and the pilots came back inside. The jet doors closed and the pilots got in the cockpit.

I almost felt as if we were in some movie where a massive super-storm was coming in and was going to suck us away if we didn't get in the air right now. I guess I'd seen too many of those movies. The runway better not crack open as we were about to take off. I didn't need to be sucked into some hole in the middle of the Earth.

My heart began to beat a little faster as the plane started to move onto the runway. Another plane, which was in front of us, took off as we waited for them to get far enough away before we could get out there. I gripped the armrests like last time as Blake tried to comfort me and keep me calm.

I took a sip of water before setting it in the holder, as I could hear the engines starting to really turn on. This was it. Keep it together, Penny. You can do this.

The plane hit full speed and started to thunder down the runway. I could feel my teeth chattering as I kept my eyes clenched closed. We lifted off, the roaring of the landing gear against the runway quickly disappearing, as I kept my eyes closed and swore not to open them.

"It's okay. We're up," Blake said a few minutes later, as he put his hand on my knee.

I opened my eyes and saw little black specks from keeping them closed so hard. As I blinked a few times they started to go away, and I looked out the window and down at the world below. I had to admit that it was beautiful, even if it was absolutely frightening. To think that we, as humans, were soaring above the clouds made me realize how insignificant I really was in the grand scheme of it all.

After two hours and a short nap later, we landed in San Francisco, right back where it all began yesterday morning. I told Blake I had some homework I had to do when he asked me to come over and stay the night, and he understood and asked if I would stay over tomorrow night. He said he had some things to talk to me about, and I thought I knew what he wanted. I wasn't sure why he waited until *after* our romantic trip, but I knew it was going to happen soon. I just hoped I was ready for what might be coming next.

CHAPTER SIXTEEN

Blake

I hated waking up without Penny in my arms. It was almost unbearable and something that I should never have had to go through again. My life felt so empty without her directly in it, and I wanted that to change. That was why I asked her over last night, though she couldn't come. After our trip together, I wanted to make things official. I wanted to look her in the eyes, muster up some courage, and ask her for the thing that would make me, and hopefully her, happiest of all. I wanted her to be my girlfriend.

I'd never been so sure of something in my life. Before her, I fucked women senseless before letting them go and getting on with my life. I never thought of settling down, at least not anytime soon, but life threw a major curveball at me the day she showed up in my offices. It was like I knew then and there something was special about her, even if I didn't know a relationship would be that thing. I acted all macho and cunning when we first went out, but over time that faded and I was left being the type of person she made me be. I was a *better* person, and one who valued having a partner there to do anything and everything with, no matter how big or small.

I couldn't wait until she came over later tonight and once again was pressed into my arms. She'd fall asleep, though I'd do nothing about it. I couldn't wait until she came and kissed me softly as she tugged at the top of my shirt to pull me in just a little harder. I couldn't wait until I had it all, and I couldn't wait until I had *her*.

I texted her sweet things to wake up to, as I knew she'd never be caught dead up this early in the morning. While I got dressed I thought about how I'd go about this later tonight. How would I ask her? I knew it wasn't a marriage proposal or anything crazy, but I still wanted it to be nice and special. I didn't want to just come out with it and ask her like some teenage boy who had no idea how to speak to a woman. I wanted her to swoon and feel butterflies, just like I'd feel my own stomach tickle a little bit.

The only way I knew how, at least in the apartment, was during a dinner—a romantic one. I'd get candles, dim the lights, get some roses, and the best takeout I could find. We'd crack open a bottle of wine, eat, and have a wonderful conversation before I segued into the question that might set off the rest of my life—our lives—together.

I checked my phone as I got my things together to leave. She hadn't replied yet, which I expected, though I'd hoped I'd be wrong. I put on my suit jacket, grabbed my wallet, keys, and phone, and headed out the door and down the elevator to my waiting car.

"Good morning, sir. I take it your trip went flawlessly?" Gustav asked.

"It did, Gustav. The meetings were taken care of and we're on track now," I said.

"And how about your time with Penny, sir?" Gustav asked.

"It couldn't have been better. She's a great girl," I said, as I got into the car.

As we pulled close to the building and sat at the stoplight, a notification from Penny came up on my phone. I opened it, seeing a smiley face, as she said good morning back and that she was excited to see me tonight. There was nothing better than starting my day off right with words like those from the only woman who mattered to me.

Even though tonight was going to be a bit nerve-wracking, I knew things were only going to get better from here. I was finally going to have her officially, and I couldn't have been more excited.

CHAPTER SEVENTEEN

Penelope

I felt anxious for the majority of the day. What was I going to do? I obviously knew what Blake wanted to ask me and talk to me about, I wasn't stupid, but how should I go about getting across what I had to say? Should I come out with it right away? Should I stop him right before he talked and come clean? What I did wasn't *that* bad, was it? I didn't even think it was, but I didn't feel right not being honest with him before entering something as serious as a committed, monogamous relationship.

I knew I couldn't tell him over text right now to get it over with. It wouldn't be right. I had to look into his eyes and say that at first, after we started talking again, I used him for material things and sex. He'd bought me groceries a few times, I used Gustav,

I went on a trip with him, I fucked him a couple times, and so much more. I wasn't doing it to be malicious, at least not in my eyes, but rather to just really drill into his head what it felt like for me to be used. What I'd done wasn't even as bad as what he'd done, either, or at least I thought so. I hoped I wasn't just trying to justify it in my head so I could believe what I was telling him. Hell, maybe he'd believe it.

When I got home later that night, I had the entire apartment to myself. I took a long shower, as some of my best thinking came when I was in there, and got myself ready as I put on more makeup than usual and made sure to do my hair. He couldn't say no to this face. At least, I hoped so.

"So, tonight's the night, huh?" Nicolette asked, as I came out of the bathroom completely ready.

"Yeah, tonight's the night. I'm finally coming clean," I said.

"You don't have to do that, you know. You could just, I don't know, keep it a secret and not ruin a great thing," she said.

"I have to be honest with him," I said.

"What if honesty makes you lose him? You barely even did anything and besides, you don't want to ruin what could be the greatest relationship of your life over something as stupid as this. Think about it," she said, before going into her room.

I'd thought about it a million times, and every single time I came up with the same answer. I couldn't justify lying to him, and I definitely didn't want to keep anything from him. I wanted him to know before he asked me to be his girlfriend so I wouldn't feel like anything was hanging over my head. I wanted him to know the truth before he did something I knew was very hard for him to do.

Gustav was waiting outside my apartment as I came downstairs in the nice black dress Blake liked so much. I still had my clothes over there just in case he forgave me and wanted me to stay, but I wasn't holding my breath. I knew it could be a long shot.

I got in the car and Gustav drove off, as I must've looked a little anxious and flustered in the back seat. I tapped my fingers on the armrest, feeling nauseous.

"Everything okay?" he asked, as he looked at me in the rearview mirror.

"Yeah, just a little nervous," I said.

"Everything will go okay, Penny. I know it," he said.

I didn't know if he knew about the upcoming question, so I just smiled and nodded politely before going back to my own worry and fear. Every block we passed on the way to Blake's apartment made the realization of what was coming more and more clear. Here I was, a proverbial pig going to the slaughter, and I could've, and still could, prevent it. Why was I such a glutton for punishment? Why did I have to be so good? Why couldn't I just be like Nicolette and say screw it? Fuck my moral compass.

We pulled into Blake's garage and Gustav parked before coming around and opening my door. He said to have a good night and I politely returned the well wishes, as I couldn't even be conscious enough to ask about his family. I was too self-absorbed to worry about anyone else.

Blake buzzed me up and I got into the elevator before taking a deep breath, letting it out slowly, and pressing the "close" button on the doors. Up I went, looking at the floor icon above the door, before it stopped at his floor. The doors opened, and Blake and an amazing sight awaited me.

The apartment was dimly lit and I saw candles flickering in the distance, standing tall around the table. Rose petals were scattered about, forming a long, narrow path towards the table, where I could see dishes and wine on ice. Blake came towards me, kissing me softly, as he hugged me and gave me chills. He did all this for me? Did he think this was a marriage proposal? No, I couldn't think like that. This was the nicest thing any guy had ever done for me, and it meant the world that he'd go through this much trouble. I would've been just as happy on the pier with a corn dog and a few grunts asking me to be his girlfriend.

"I feel like I haven't seen you in forever, and I just saw you yesterday," he said, putting his arm around me as we walked towards the table.

"Yeah, I know what you mean. I think about you a lot when we're not together," I said.

My compliments had two motivations. I did think about him a lot when we were apart, and I would never lie to him through the compliments I gave him, but I was also trying to sweeten him up. Maybe it would lessen the blow and keep me safer.

"I had dinner prepared. Are you hungry?" he asked.

"Yeah, I'm starved," I said.

I decided to wait until I thought the time was right before telling him anything. Maybe filling his stomach and getting a little booze in him would be the right way to go. Then he likely wouldn't be as mad. Besides, I wasn't ready to leave right after getting here, should it go that badly.

Blake pulled out my chair for me, which almost felt like a little dig, as I tried to keep my composure. I sat down and he scooted it in, and then he grabbed the bottle of wine and poured us two glasses. He sat down, looked me in the eyes, and smiled, which calmed me down internally just a little.

"So, how was your day?" he asked.

"It went well. I did some homework and quizzes online that I missed during the trip," I said.

"I hope it wasn't too much of an inconvenience," he said.

"Not at all. I don't mind the online quizzes too much. It's a lot better being in bed than sitting in a hard chair in a classroom with a bunch of other people around. It's nice," I said.

"Yeah, I didn't get to take anything online. Everything was turned in physically, but I think that's more because of the professors I had. We had an early version of the online software for colleges, but it wasn't widely used, at least where I went. I'm glad you get to experience it, though," he said.

I skimmed my fork against the buttery mashed potatoes to get a wisp of it and stuck it in my mouth. With my other hand planted firmly in my lap, I felt a bit of nerves as he smiled at me while he chewed. I almost feared that it was about to come back up. It was the reason why I wasn't taking big bites. I wanted to be able to cut him off should it arise.

We went through our entire meal sipping wine, taking bites, and forgoing any topics even closely related to dating, a relationship, or where we stood. Were my instincts wrong about tonight? Did he have something else on his mind? Was I in the clear—at least for now? I couldn't be. I wasn't that lucky.

After we finished our meal, Blake suggested we go over to the couch, light a fire, and look out over the city lights. I agreed, and with the lights still dim, he pressed a button on his fireplace and it lit up, the flames dancing along glass shards that sat inside. With the overall lights dim, we could see out all over the city as his floor-to-ceiling windows acted as brilliant frames showcasing the urban landscape.

Blake set his wine glass down on the table and I followed. He coughed a little, though in a nervous tone, as my stomach did flip-flops, and I was sure I was starting to get a rash on my chest. I couldn't see it, but I'd be damned surprised if somebody hadn't rubbed poison ivy all over me, because I was itchier than I'd ever been before.

"I wanted to talk to you about something tonight," he said.

Was this it? Was it coming? I knew I had to make sure before I spurted anything out.

"Yeah? What about?" I asked, my voice cracking.

"About us, and where we're headed," he said.

Shit. He *was* going there. I almost couldn't speak, but I knew I needed to spit something out. He looked at me, the fire twinkling in his gorgeous eyes, before I finally got it out, right as his mouth opened to speak.

"Wait," I said, causing him to look at me weirdly.

"What?" he asked.

"I need to tell you something," I said.

"You're not a man, are you?" he asked.

"What?" I asked.

"Sorry, I saw it once in a movie," he said.

"I'm a woman, but before you go any further, and I think I know where you're headed, I need to stop you and tell you something," I said.

"You're not interested in dating, are you?" he asked.

"What? No, that's not it at all," I said.

"Then you should hear what I have to say before giving your answer," he said.

"I can't do that. I need to be honest with you. After you hurt me at the gala, well, after Tom hurt me, really, I never thought I'd recover. You used me, lied to me, and most of all, hurt me. I never thought I'd see you again, at least not this soon, but then fate happened and we ended up reconnecting and getting to the point we're at now. That's what makes this hard," I said.

He looked at me with a confused expression, and I could tell he was clearly nervous.

"When you first contacted me again, and we talked, people told me I should do to you what you did to me. They said I should use you to get some things that I wanted so you'd know how it felt for me. I hated the idea, I really did, but something about it stuck with me. Here you were, just after tricking me, and you really were going to face no repercussions other than being without me for a short while, and even that wasn't really *that* long," I said.

"So you were using me this entire time since we got back together?" he asked.

"No, not entirely. I got a few things out of you, or tried, rather, but I couldn't get myself to do it all the way. I'm not the type of person to try to hurt you even though you really hurt me. Over time you showed me the type of guy you really are, the sweet guy who's here with me now, and I forgot all about what I was doing. I was just being with you and nothing else. I was reminded of everything, though, and I couldn't just let you go on without knowing. I had to tell you so I could get the weight off of my chest and my heart. I was going to do it before you asked me to be your girlfriend, which I think was coming, and I thought you'd do that in Seattle, but you never did," I said.

Blake looked a little confused and slightly hurt as he sat there and tried to process what I'd said. He didn't look at me, didn't hold my hand, and didn't try to get close at all. I was afraid this would happen. I was afraid he'd be pushed so far back that we'd never recover. I should've just listened to Nicolette. I should've taken this to my grave.

"So, you used me? Is that what you're ultimately saying?" he asked.

"At the beginning, yes, both sexually and for a couple things. But I don't think it's anything close to what you did to me," I said.

"You can't keep using what I did against me, Penelope. I know what I did was wrong, but you know I regretted it and it wasn't like that the entire time. I thought you forgave me," he said.

"I did, I do, and that's why I wish you'd forgive me for this," I said, as tears started to stream down my cheeks.

"On one hand I want to be mad at you, but on the other I feel like I'm gridlocked, and I can't. You basically got even with me, got back at me, and I deserve it for what I did, but I can't shake it. I was going to ask you the one thing I haven't asked in years. I was going to ask you to be my girlfriend, and to completely change myself for you. I was going to commit myself to *you*," he said.

"And you still can. I want to be with you, Blake. I want to so badly," I said.

"I don't know, Penelope. I don't know anymore," he said, before standing up and walking around the table.

"Where are you going?" I asked, as I got up and followed him.

He went into his refrigerator and pulled out a bottle of water before taking a few chugs of it and tossing it in the trash. He looked distraught and hurt, and worst of all, it was because of me.

"I don't think I can ask you that question anymore. At least not now," he said, with his hand to his forehead.

"So that's it? We're over?" I asked, as I couldn't hold my flood of tears back any longer.

"I don't know. I think I just need some time to

process all this. I think that would be best," he said, before looking up at me.

"I guess I'll get my things and leave," I said.

"I'll contact you when I'm ready to talk about this. Until then, please take care of yourself. I still care about you, a lot, but this back and forth thing that we've had with me hurting you, and then you getting revenge, and now being here, is just too much to process right now," he said.

"Before I go, I just want you to know that it was all a mistake. I didn't *use* you like you think. I got a few things, and you know I never ask for anything, and I used you for sex at the beginning. You're the only guy I think about and the only guy I want, and if you choose to leave, you should know you'll always be the one who got away to me. I'm sorry," I said, before walking back over to the elevator and getting inside.

Blake watched me as the doors closed. I broke down with my back against the cold elevator wall and felt my face and body tense up like never before. I knew he was going to be pissed, but I never expected this. I didn't think he could get this mad, even if I was a little scared of it before. I thought he'd be mad at me for a few days and then get over it. But I was wrong—dead wrong.

Nicolette wasn't there when I got home, which was all the better. I didn't text her, didn't call her, but left a note taped to her bedroom door letting her know I was here and sleeping and to not wake me. I closed my bedroom door, put a bottle of water on my nightstand, got changed into my pajamas, and sat on the edge of my bed with a little lamp illuminating my room.

I put my hands against my face, rubbed it slowly, and took a few deep breaths as I tried to calm myself down enough to lie down.

I did, with my phone at my side, periodically checking it just in case Blake texted me and I didn't hear the notification. He never did. As I opened my photos app and scrolled through his selfies and our pictures together, I couldn't help but feel like I'd lost a piece of myself.

I knew this wasn't, and couldn't, be the end to our story. I knew this was just another hurdle we had to overcome that would make a great story one day. I knew I wanted to be with him and nobody else, and it wasn't for his net worth and the things he had. I was falling for this man, and I wasn't going to just let him leave me behind and move on with his life. I was going to salvage whatever I could, and we were going to come back stronger than ever.

I was sure of this, and I was sure of us.

Did you like this title? If so, please consider leaving a review. It will help not only me as the author grow, but will also let other readers know your thoughts and opinions.

Want to receive the first three volumes of my serial series The Stipulation for free? Sign up for my mailing list below and have them delivered right to your inbox. You'll receive new book notifications, free books, giveaways, and much more!

http://eepurl.com/bb6VVb

ABOUT THE AUTHOR

M.L. Young is a New Adult Romance author currently residing in northern Illinois. When not writing, she enjoys horseback riding, sewing, and dreaming about the hot guys she writes about in her books.

M.L. loves interacting with fans, so interact with her! You can find her on Facebook, Twitter, and through e-mail!

www.facebook.com/realmlyoung

www.twitter.com/realmlyoung

www.authormlyoung.com

15045323R00120

Printed in Great Britain
by Amazon